MUSEUM of the WEIRD

ELINA EATING FLOWER SEEDS

POST-APOCALYPTIC ROLEX

ARMADILLO WITH MILLER HIGH LIFE

HUMAN TONGUE SAUTÉED IN BUTTERMILK

JEW

FC2

Tuscaloosa

Copyright © 2010 by Amelia Gray
The University of Alabama Press
Tuscaloosa, Alabama 35487-0380
All rights reserved
First edition

Published by FC2, an imprint of The University of Alabama Press, with support
provided by the Publishing Program at the University of Houston–Victoria.

Address all editorial inquiries to: Fiction Collective Two, University of Houston–
Victoria, School of Arts and Sciences, Victoria, TX 77901-5731

Cover Design: Zach Dodson at bleachedwhale.com
Typography: Kyle Schlesinger and the Publishing Program at UHV
Typeface: Adobe Garamond Pro
Produced and printed in the United States of America

∞

The paper on which this book is printed meets the minimum requirements of
American National Standard for Information Sciences—Permanence of Paper
for Printed Library Materials, ANSI Z39.48-1984

Library of Congress Cataloging-in-Publication Data
Gray, Amelia, 1982–
Museum of the weird / Amelia Gray.
    p. cm.
ISBN: 978-1-57366-156-0 (pbk. : alk. paper)—ISBN: 978-1-57366-818-7
(electronic)
I. Title.
PS3607.R387M87 2010
813'. 6—dc22
                                                              2009041859

For my parents

ACKNOWLEDGEMENTS

Grateful acknowledgement is made to the following publications in which these stories first appeared: "Babies" in *Guernica* and *The Austin Anthology: Emerging Writers of Central Texas*; "Trip Advisory: The Boyhood Home of Former President Ronald Reagan" in *McSweeney's Internet Tendency*; "This Quiet Complex" in *Monkeybicycle*; "The Cottage Cheese Diet" and "There Will Be Sense" in *DIAGRAM*; "Code of Operation: Snake Farm" and "The Cube" in *Spork*; "A Javelina Story" in *Bust Down the Door and Eat All the Chickens*; "The Picture Window" and "Fish" in *Keyhole Magazine*; "The Darkness" and "The Tortoise and the Hare" (as "Beating the Odds") in *Dispatch Litareview*; "Waste" in *Annalemma Magazine*; "Love, Mortar" in *Bound Off*; "Death of a Beast" in *Juked*; "Diary of the Blockage" in *Caketrain*; "Vultures" in *Swivel*; "The Movement" in *Storyglossia*; "Dinner" in *Shelf Life Magazine*; "The Vanished" in *Sleepingfish;* "The Suitcase" in *The Sonora Review;* ; and "Thoughts While Strolling" in *Alice Blue Review.*

Gratitude is owed to Featherproof Books, Justin Boyle, Carmen Edington, Jon Knutson, and the kids in the van.

CONTENTS

CONTENTS

BABIES

One morning, I woke to discover I had given birth overnight. It was troubling to realize because I had felt no pain as I slept, did not remember the birth, and in fact had not even known I was pregnant. But there he was, a little baby boy, swaddled among cotton sheets, sticky with amniotic fluid and other various baby-goops. The child had pulled himself up to my breast in the night and was at that moment having breakfast. He looked up and smiled when I reached for him.

"Hello," I said.

I bundled my sheets and my mattress pad into a trash bag and set it by the door. I got into the shower with my new baby, because we were both covered in the material of his birth and were becoming cold. I soaped him up with my gentle face soap. He laughed and I laughed, because using face soap on an infant is funny. I toweled him off and wrapped him in a linen shirt.

On the walk to the store, I called my boyfriend, Chuck.

"I had a baby overnight," I said.

Chuck coughed. "I am not amenable to babies," he said.

I looked down at the baby. He was bundled up in the fine shirt and smiled as if he was aware of the quality of the shirt, and enjoyed it. "I am in love with this baby," I said, "and that's that."

At the grocery, I bought baby powder, diapers, two pacifiers, and a box of chocolate. I walked us home, fit a diaper on the baby, and ate a piece of chocolate. Chuck came over and said that perhaps he was amenable to babies after all, and we fell asleep together with the baby between us. The baby had not cried all day and neither had I.

The next morning, we woke to discover I had once again given birth, this time to a little girl. The babies were nestled together between us on the bed, and my spare sheets were ruined. I handed the babies off to Chuck and sent him to the shower. I bundled up the spare sheets and placed them by the other bag of sheets. Then, I got into the shower with Chuck. It was a nervous fit, with the two of us and the babies.

"These babies are so quiet," said Chuck. "I love them, too. But I hope you don't have another one overnight."

We all had a good laugh. The next morning, there was another baby. And another. And another. And another.

And that brings us to today.

WASTE

Roger's assigned route had him picking up medical waste at most of the plastic surgery offices in town. He smelled it on his skin by the end of the day. The plastic surgery places were less of a hassle than the hospital and worlds away from the free clinic. After a day full of sharps and used lipo tubes and ruptured implants and the weight of discarded flesh, he tried not to think about the contents of the barrels. He sometimes wore his nose-plug at home.

The long shower he took after work helped a little, and it was good to finally smell the world around him as he dried himself off. From where he stood in his bedroom he could smell the dust in the carpet, the vinegar smell of his freshly washed windows, and the wooden bed frame. He detected the slightest hint of mold in the wall, which didn't surprise him, as the duplex was fifty years old at least and sagging. After a good rain, the mold smelled damp and sweet.

Roger enjoyed his evenings when Olive, his neighbor on the other side of the duplex, was cooking. Olive worked as a line cook at a vegetarian restaurant and spent her evenings frying meat. The smells slipped under the door connecting their apartments and seeped out of closed windows to surround the house. One night, Roger smelled something new and knocked on their connecting door.

"Hello, nose," Olive said. "It's chorizo." Behind her, a sauté pan sizzled with orange meat.

"My grandmother made that in the morning," Roger said.

Olive leaned against the doorjamb. She was still wearing her hairnet from work. "Probably with eggs," she said.

"And cheese, and corn chips sometimes."

"A fine breakfast." She gestured towards the pan with the spatula. "I'm making hamburgers. I mix it with ground chuck. I have enough for another one, if you want."

They sat on the floor to eat. The meat soaked orange fat into the bread. The two of them worked through a thick pile of napkins. Olive's apron was a cornflower blue hospital gown that Roger had picked up for her months ago. Her skin looked pale next to it.

"You have a lovely collarbone," Roger said.

She looked at him. "Lymph nodes," she said. "And salivary glands." She took a bite and chewed thoughtfully. "They make chorizo with the lymph nodes and salivary glands of the pig. Cheeks, sometimes."

He swallowed. "Cheeks."

"Pig to pork," Olive said. "When does the change happen? At death, it's a dead pig. At the market, it's a pork product. But when does the grand transformation take place? After the animal's last breath? When it's wrapped and packed?"

"It would be horrible to be wrapped and packed."

Olive shrugged. "Some might think so. The pig might think so, if it wasn't well on its way to becoming pork. But it's lucky, in a way. Not everything gets to transform." Her collarbone ducked in and out of the neck of her hospital gown as she talked.

Roger returned his sandwich to its plate. "I'm going to have the rest of this at work tomorrow," he said.

She unlocked her side of the connecting door for him. "Think about it," she said. "The pig gets to become pork. The rest of us simply go from live body to dead body."

***

At work, Roger loaded bags into heavy drums and wheeled the drums from the loading dock to his truck using a dolly and securing straps. He rolled the drums onto the truck's hydraulic lift, operated the lift, and drove to the next office and eventually to the incinerator. The metal drums warmed in the sun in the bed of the truck.

One of the big autoclaves was broken at the sterilization plant, and he got to take his time on his last pickups. He talked to the nurses and drove aimlessly around town. He sat at a covered picnic table five hundred feet from his truck and ate a late lunch. The chorizo had solidified in the fridge overnight, giving the burger neon orange spots. Roger removed the nose-plug and clipped the lanyard to the lapel of his jumpsuit.

When he was young, one of his teachers in grade school showed the class a video of a slaughterhouse. It began slowly, the picture grainy and unclear, the storyline featuring frowning men in white lab coats and packages of meat on a store shelf, but a brief segment at the middle of the video showed the actual process of the killing; the animals screaming and bleeding between metal railings, their heads swinging.

Roger couldn't remember what type of animal was featured. He was in the fourth grade, and one of the girls in the class threw up in a trashcan next to the teacher's desk. Roger watched her. He took a pencil out of his plastic pencil case and drove it slowly into his hand. The graphite left a black mark on his palm, ringed with purple. The teacher was fired later that month.

As he ate his lunch, Roger decided that the pig never turned into pork. The pig was always pork, from the moment it was born into the world.

***

The hot water ran out at home that evening and Roger shivered as he rinsed his hair. He dressed and knocked on Olive's door. She was wearing her hospital gown and had a towel wrapped around her head.

"So that's where the hot water went," she said, tousling his wet hair.

"The pig was always pork," said Roger.

Olive thought about it. "I want to show you something," she said. "But you can't tell anyone. And you have to wait while I change."

"Okay," he said.

She was still wearing the hospital gown when she opened the door again to invite him in. The gown was cinched with a silver belt. She was holding a shoebox.

"You can't tell anyone," she said. "This is illegal." She opened the box. Inside was a clear plastic bag, with a small brown object that looked like a dried mushroom. Olive shook the box gently, as if it might come alive.

"Tongue," she said. "An actual tongue, from a person."

Roger touched the edge of the shoebox, and then shoved his hands into his pockets. "Really," he said.

"The real deal," she said. "Cost me a fortune. It's from this freaked-out monastery where the monks cut out their own tongues to get closer to God. They dehydrate them and sell them for two thousand per. Luckily, I know a guy. I've been saving all year to get one. Apparently they're like pâté."

Roger bit his own tongue, gently, at the thought.

Olive took the box into the kitchen and set it on the counter, next to a white bowl filled with a white liquid. "Buttermilk with a dash of vinegar," she said. She opened the bag and dropped the tongue into the bowl without ceremony. "Takes the bitterness out of game. Just a little dunk before the flour. I'm not sure we're gamey but I thought I'd give it a shot." She set a pan to heat on the range and dropped two pats of butter into the pan. "I believe I shall sauté," she said.

Roger looked around Olive's apartment. There were roach motels lining their shared wall, an old city map covering a foundation crack next to her bedroom door.

"Did you hear about the Japanese cannibal they caught?" Roger asked. "He told the court what people taste like."

Olive turned and leaned on the counter.

"Sushi," he said.

She picked three bowls out of the dishwasher. She cracked eggs into one bowl, poured flour into another, and bread crumbs into a third. She sliced a clove of garlic and dropped the slices into the pan.

"Tuna," Roger said.

"You should stay for dinner." She poured him a glass of wine. "This is a really special night," she said, pouring her own glass. "I'm glad to share it with someone."

"I'm glad to be here," Roger said. He sat down on the floor, holding his glass with both hands.

"Don't be nervous," Olive said. "You can have a little bite, and if you don't like it, I'll eat the rest. Culinary adventure." She fished around in the buttermilk for the tongue, and dropped it first in the flour, then the eggs, then the breadcrumbs.

"I've never had pâté," Roger said.

"Liverwurst?"

He shook his head.

"You should try it," she said. "Hell of a meat. You're eating the energy of an animal. It used to be this strong, busy liver. All that energy is contained in a tiny thing."

"The tongue is a busy organ."

In the ensuing silence, Roger drank half his wine.

"That's the idea behind it," Olive said, washing her hands in the sink.

The garlic grew fragrant in the butter. Olive dried her hands and used a fork to drop the tongues into the pan.

"I feel like I should cross myself," she said.

Roger was still thinking about Olive's tongue.

When the tongue was done, she plated it simply, between lines of wasabi and chili sauces. "A little spice," she said. They shared the plate together on the floor. Her knives were sharp. Olive declared the meat to be closer to liverwurst than pâté. Roger chewed thoughtfully. His own tongue touched the tongue he was eating. He felt strange.

"A strong meat," she said, finishing the last bite.

"I was thinking we could go out to eat sometime," Roger said. "Somewhere nice."

She looked at his plate. "You didn't finish your half," she said.

"It was okay. Do you want it?"

"Two thousand dollars," she said, spearing his half. "A rare treat."

Roger put both palms on the ground and pushed himself up. "Thank you for dinner," he said.

The light was brighter on his side. He smelled the roach motels, the mold in the walls, and the dust in his carpet.

"We'll work on you," she said, through the closed door.

"I appreciate that," he said quietly, because he wasn't sure she was talking to him. She didn't respond. He turned off all the lights and did not turn them on again for three days.

The sanitizing facility where Roger collected trash could process five million pounds of waste a year. After sanitation, the waste was taken by another set of trucks to the landfill, eight tons at a time, then sanitized and shredded, then dumped and compacted and picked through by seagulls.

The rusty barrels were almost too warm to touch by sunset. He loaded each onto the dolly, wheeled the dolly to the hydraulic lift, pressed the button that lifted them into the truck, and rolled them from the lift to the truck bed. He found it difficult to work without thinking about the contents of the drums. The needles, the gauze, the hot, moving mass of lipids and grafts, of broken or rejected skin, punctuated by shards of bone. The bone was like raisins in a cake.

On the way home, he bought a roll of liverwurst and a bouquet of flowers. He wasn't sure which color Olive would like and picked white lilies because they looked the freshest. It had been a long time since Roger brought anyone flowers. The cashier covered her mouth when he passed through her line, and Roger remembered after that he must have smelled terrible.

After his shower, he put the liverwurst in the refrigerator, picked a wilted petal off the lilies, and knocked on the connecting door. At first, there was no response. He held his ear to the door and didn't hear anything. The door smelled like rot and wood and paint. He knocked again.

"Roger," she said, from the other side. "Come in."

Olive's silver belt made her look segmented. Her white legs stretched out like a child's and she was leaning against the far wall, underneath the old map of a city Roger didn't recognize. The crack in the wall, the one the map only partly covered, stretched down to her head, making it look like she was attached. Her left foot was bleeding through a wide swath of bandages onto the tarp it was resting on. The bowl next to her was full of blood.

Olive looked a little pale. "I don't think I should move," she said.

"What are you doing?" Roger shut the door behind him and stood with his back to it.

"I decided I might try and eat my toes," Olive said, closing her eyes. "But now that I've started, I don't think I should move."

Roger pushed himself off the wall and knelt down next to her. He unbuckled her silver belt and reached with it under her dress. He looped the belt around the top of her leg and tightened it. His hands were not shaking.

"Sit on the loose end," he said, pushing it under her. "I hope that works."

"You brought flowers," she said, blinking.

"Olive," he said. "You cut off your toes."

She looked down at the bowl. "Are they still toes?" she asked.

He thought about the metal drums heating in the sun, bouncing in the back of the truck as he paraded their human contents across town. "I don't want to look at them," he said.

She touched her leg. "Let's drink grapefruit juice," she said.

"We should really get you to the hospital."

The metal drums, hot blood clinging to moist gauze pads.

"I'm thirsty," she said.

"You have no toes on your left foot."

"I'm thirsty," she said. She looked at him. She seemed very reasonable.

"A little juice," Roger said. "And then straight to the hospital."

She nodded and motioned to the kitchen, where Roger filled two glasses with juice.

"I was considering a stew," she said. He put a glass of juice into her hand on her lap, wrapped her fingers around it. "Chop, braise, stew. I bought the carrots this morning. I already had potatoes and broth. You would need a bit of flour first, and butter. I have those, too."

The juice glass trembled and spilled onto her lap. "Cooking makes me feel better," she said.

He looked around for another bandage for her foot. "I don't cook," he said.

"I can't feel my leg."

"That's normal."

"You should try it," she said. "Cooking. Then we'll go."

Roger sat back on his heels. He was worried, but proud of himself for remembering proper tourniquet procedure. He had saved her life. She might thank him once she was in a better frame of mind.

She raised her head and shook it, opening her eyes briefly before closing them again. "A stew," she said. "I promise, after stew."

"I don't know how," he said, but she didn't seem to hear him. He picked up the flowers he had brought her, ruined now, though when he put them in the sink they still brightened the room.

UNSOLVED MYSTERY

My first week on the force and that crazy guy starts killing men, digging into the chest cavity—with an actual bonesaw, we think, the cut is so clean—and removing a rib. We nickname him God to be real clever. My girl Lisa thinks I'm joking when I tell her this and when I insist it's true, she throws me out. The devout type; I should have known. Meanwhile this guy's on the loose and looking for victims. Usually homeless guys. We found one last week in an alley, frozen to his own blood and stuck to the ground. No calling card from God, just a wound that looks like a shotgun blast at first and more gruesome on closer inspection.

And that's another thing—no other marks. I can't figure it. We run toxicology tests. We go over them with a blacklight, we check every inch of skin and hair with agonizing precision. Sam, the morgue tech, says precision in this business is usually agonizing. No strangle marks, no bruises, no chemicals beyond the ones typically cruising through a bum's veins. No organs harvested. I half expect these guys stitched up, it's such a clean job. Other than the blood, I mean. Sam says it's divinity, or a spell, but I think that's bull. I think it's cold in those alleys, and God is working fast.

Two things happen to bust everything wide open. This sicko, he gets a guy in a house. He gets him, safe and warm, in his own bed at night. This will baffle me when I find out about it but I don't learn about it when the other guys do, because my girl Lisa chose that moment to pull a sneak attack on me and bring a priest home for dinner. Some poor sap is missing a rib, bleeding out on his 350 thread-count Egyptian cotton, and I'm passing the asparagus to a guy in a plastic collar.

***

This is Father Matthew, Lisa says. She serves fish sticks with mayo and pours the iced tea. Father Matthew spends some time looking pleased with himself. He says, Lisa's been telling me some interesting things about this case you're working on.

I say, Yeah. I say Listen, the boys aren't sure it's a serial case yet and we don't want copycats, so don't leak it to the press or anything.

Father Matthew holds up his hands. He says, What is going on with this world.

I tell him, This guy God, he's got a bonesaw on loan and he's cutting into men and taking their ribs. Homeless guys.

Bonesaw? says Lisa, dipping a fish stick into a pile of mayo.

And he calls himself God, Father Matthew says.

Yeah, I say. Well, tell the truth, that's what us guys down at the precinct are calling him. Kind of a code name, you know.

Nobody knows his true name, Father Matthew says.

I say, Yeah.

He puts down his glass, says, Naming God is a very serious thing.

Yeah well, I say, He's everywhere, right?

Sure, he says.

Even in serial killers, right?

AMELIA GRAY

I thought you didn't know he was a serial killer, Lisa says.

Father Matthew holds the edge of the table. It's not a name you just throw around, he says. It makes it sound like you respect him.

After Father Matthew leaves, I do the dishes for Lisa and crawl into bed just as she's finishing her vespers. All the doors are locked, the windows are bolted, and I have a chair propped against the front door. Just in case God's watching and he wants to make it personal.

We're safe, Lisa says. I asked for protection.

He won't get in tonight, I say.

She says, I think you worried Father Matthew a little with the respect thing. She kisses me on the cheek.

Worried myself a little, I say, truthfully. What I don't say is, God's a clever bastard and I do respect him. He's everywhere.

DINNER

When the waiter brought a plate of hair to the table alongside Beth's soup, it was difficult to be polite about it. Still, Beth felt the need to be polite, because it was a nice restaurant, and she was on a date for the first time in months, and with a guy she actually liked. His name was Dave and he smelled like shaving cream and the subway.

From the way Dave looked first at the plate of hair and then at her, Beth couldn't be sure if he had ordered it for her, as a surprise, while she was in the bathroom. He had been talking earlier about the exotic locations he had visited in the previous year—Bali, Peru, some island near Madagascar—and she assumed that interesting foods and customs were a part of those voyages. Dave had a disarming smile and an easy way with words that had made the night go quickly until that moment.

Beth dipped her spoon into the soup, a tomato-cream bisque that she had ordered with a sidelong glance at Dave, hoping he wouldn't think her uncultured for skipping over the more adventurous carrot ginger gazpacho. Dave had ordered a salad, which had not yet arrived, giving him time to focus his gaze on her. She put her spoon down.

"Please," Dave said. "Eat. Don't wait for me."

"Would you like to try anything?" Beth said. She hoped Dave would go for the hair, which lay clumped on its plate directly between them. In fact, it wouldn't be entirely clear that the plate of hair was meant for her, except that the waiter had bowed at her when delivering the plate, and had murmured to her his wishes that she enjoy her meal; despite, she assumed, the fact that her entree of squab would be arriving later. Beth wondered for an uneasy moment if squab was not actually a small bird, as she had figured, but a plate of hair.

"Do try something," she said.

Dave shook his head. He was still smiling, but his gaze had dropped to her lips, meaning either that he wanted to kiss her— she had read about this technique in magazines—or that he wanted her to take a healthy chunk of hair with her fork and choke it down with a swallow of red wine, forcing the clogged mass down her throat like an obstruction through the pipes of a bathtub.

Beth couldn't take her eyes away from the plate of hair. The soup fell into the background, harboring her forgotten spoon. It was auburn hair, and piled up with a volume that made it seem as if the chef had snipped off a massive tangle and laid it there without presentation.

"Would you like to leave?" Dave asked.

It was as if he had plucked the thought from her mind, but when she looked at him, she knew it was not a sincere proposal. He had pulled some strings for their reservation, after all, getting the two of them a table at the last moment, no doubt at some expense to his professional standing. Men didn't enjoy asking for things, Beth knew from the magazines.

She shook her head at him cheerily, too quickly. She would

have to eat the hair, she knew—that or ruin the date, and everything that went along with it. He was watching. He knew it, too.

A JAVELINA STORY

The domestic hostage situation had been underway for three and a half hours, and the pack of wild animals heading up the negotiation project was making little progress. There were five javelinas and they looked intimidating enough all together, weighing as they did between fifty and eighty pounds each and brandishing tusks, trotters, and snouts. Their mottled brown hair shone with drying mud from a nearby drainage ditch. It was a warm day, with a slight breeze in the air, and the javelinas were ready for a nap.

That morning, someone at the district office made a clerical error of impressive proportions, transferring the badge status and its related responsibilities from Officer Clint Javarez to the wild javelinas. The javelinas had been found eating the fruit off a prickly pear cactus in the city park, and had spent the afternoon waiting patiently in the back of a squad car for the Animal Control van to arrive. Once the order came through, they were driven by a rookie to the site of the hostage situation, dropped at the scene with a large cardboard box of supplies, and abandoned.

Some commotion inside the building startled the javelinas

from their rest. One roused himself from their makeshift nest and trampled branches, sniffing the air. Another nosed the box, tipping its contents out in the process. From the box and into the muddy ditch rolled flares, a set of cell phones, a bullhorn, a bulletproof vest, a packet of sunflower seeds, pads of notepaper, a box of facial tissues, tear gas, five grenades, a set of walkie-talkies, and what looked to be a semi-automatic weapon. The javelinas couldn't be sure. One made a snuffling noise and trotted into the ditch to investigate.

Fifty feet away, the home's front door opened and a man's gloved hand reached out. The javelinas looked up with mild curiosity when they heard the man's voice.

"I'm losing patience in here!" the man yelled. "When I lose patience, people start getting shot in the head!" The javelinas heard screaming in the house behind the man. One of the javelinas rolled over in the nest and chewed at a knot of hair on her trotter.

The man, who was mostly obscured by the surrounding wall, held a gun in one hand and leaned the other against the door frame. "I'm trying to be reasonable!" he shouted. He switched the pistol to his other hand, knocking the barrel nervously on the door. After hearing no response, he added: "Heads will roll!"

From the ditch, the curious javelina found the sunflower seeds in their plastic packet. The javelina lay one trotter delicately at the edge of the packet, lowered his snout to the ground, and took the edge of the plastic between his teeth.

At the door, the man wiped the back of his neck with a paper towel. *The silent tactic*, he thought, remembering back to a freshman psychology book he had stolen at a yard sale and kept by his toilet. *Reverse psychology*. In the back room, his hostages were screaming again. "Shut up," he called back, "or I'll put eight rounds into your forearms!" *I could really learn something here*, he thought.

The sunflower seeds remained trapped in their packet, the slippery plastic elusive to the animal's teeth. The javelina made a trumpeting noise and drove his trotter down, first crushing a cell phone, then one of the walkie-talkies. The other beasts were alarmed and excited by the noise and tumbled down the hill in a mass. In their excitement they crushed the flares, smeared the paper into the earth, broke the sight off the rifle and bent the outer rim of the bullhorn.

The man heard the metallic crunching noises. *They're destroying their own equipment*, he thought, *but why?* He shut the door and walked into the back room, scratching the back of his head with the butt of his gun. His hostages, five fraternity brothers who the man had tied to chairs with knots he learned in the Boy Scouts, began crying and begging for their lives when they saw him.

The man raised his hand for silence. "I think we've all learned a lesson today," the man said. He raised his pistol and killed his hostages before killing himself.

Outside, the javelinas discovered that the packet of sunflower seeds had opened under the commotion of their trotters. The javelinas fell to happy fighting over the salty treats.

We have all learned a lesson today.

THE DARKNESS

"I think I'd call us strange bedfellows," the armadillo said.

The penguin barely heard her. He was, at that moment, attempting to hold a straw between his flippers.

The armadillo centered her shell on the barstool. She was drinking a Miller High Life.

"Strange bedfellows indeed," she said.

The penguin gave up on holding the straw and stood on his stool to reach the lip of the glass. He could barely wet his tongue with a little gin. "What's that?" he asked.

"You are a penguin, and I am an armadillo," the armadillo said. "My name is Betsy."

"That's a beautiful name," murmured the penguin, who was more interested in the condensation on his glass. "I fought the darkness."

"You did not."

The penguin swiveled his head to look at Betsy. He had very beady eyes.

"What's your name?" she said.

"Ray," said the penguin.

"That's a nice name."

"I fought the *fucking* darkness."

"Neat," Betsy said. She let her long tongue dip into the bottle, lapping the surface of her beer. "What was that like?"

"Well Betsy," Ray said, "it was evil incarnate."

"Oh."

"Imagine the worst evil ever done to you in your life."

Betsy thought of the time she was locked in a shed.

"Got it," she said.

Ray pecked at his highball glass in anger. "Well," he said, "imagine that, except fifteen times worse. That's what the darkness was like."

"That sounds terrible," Betsy said. She was trying to be non-committal about the whole darkness thing in the hopes that Ray would drop it. Before coming to the bar, she had used vegetable oil to shine her shell to a high sheen. In her peripheral vision, she could see the lights above the bar playing off her shoulders.

"What do you think of my shell?" she asked.

Ray leaned back a little to appraise the situation. "It's nice," he said.

"I like your coat."

"This old thing," Ray said, patting his feathers. "It'll smell like the bar for weeks. You can't get this smell out."

"That's the good thing about a shell," Betsy said.

They sat in silence. Betsy wondered if she had perhaps said too much about her shell. Ray wondered where the bartender got off serving a penguin a drink in a highball glass. He would have rather taken his gin out of an ashtray.

Betsy tapped her claw against the beer bottle. "Have you ever protected an egg?" she asked.

Ray realized that he was at the state of intoxication where anything Betsy could possibly say was going to piss him off. *Keep your cool, buddy,* he said to himself. *She's just trying to make conversation.*

"Usually that's a job for the lady penguins," Ray said. "I am a male penguin and therefore, no, I have never protected an egg."

"Right," Betsy said. "Well, I saw a documentary once, and a male penguin was protecting an egg. I figured maybe you'd have some experience."

"Sorry, I don't have any experience. I guess that makes me less of a penguin."

"I wasn't saying that."

"I suppose you think I'm some kind of *lesser* penguin, just because I fought the *fucking darkness* and tasted my own *blood,* because I haven't protected a stupid fucking *egg.*"

Betsy felt tears welling up. *Don't cry,* she said to herself. *It would be really stupid to cry at this moment.*

"I honor your fight," she said. "I did not mean to disrespect you."

Ray sank back. "It's no disrespect," he said. "I'm just a penguin in a bar, drinking my gin out of a fucking highball glass for some reason."

"I was wondering why they did that," the armadillo said.

"Doesn't make any goddamn sense," said the penguin.

THE COTTAGE CHEESE DIET

There's no reason. There's no reason why you couldn't. There's no reason it's not possible you couldn't possibly finish your mild cottage cheese breakfast, buy a ticket, take that train to the edge of the world, squeeze your eyes shut, dig the wheels into moist world-edge earth and make a dramatic plunge off the side, your friends and family waving good-bye as at the end of a parade when all that's left is sandwich wrappers and the rest of a long day, sun streaming through all the windows and still a cold room no matter how much light hits every corner, even if you take the curtains and flip them over the curtain rods so there's nothing impeding the procession of light—that kind of lazy afternoon where someone in the house mutters a promise to make banana bread but you know the bananas will spoil and cultivate bacteria, becoming dangerous like the kitchen counter you washed in your younger years first with warm water and later on with the stronger stuff, ammonia making you dizzy behind your allergen-free mask, a boiling water rinse and a layer of bleach, just a bit of the stuff mixing together into what you hear is dangerous but secretly know is a chemical so powerful that certain entities don't want you to hear about it, and by "certain entities" you mean the government, these powers in power have other plans for you but you're one step ahead, you and your sleeves with the tricks in them and your special diet, the cottage cheese diet, the diet with cottage cheese, and as you eat the cottage cheese you hold very gently on your tongue the cottages and the people inside the cottages and the people are screaming.

DEATH OF A BEAST

June was sitting at her desk and looking out the window, as she often did when she was thinking about her problems. It was a cold day, and cloudy, threatening rain. As she thought, June twisted a length of hair around and around her index finger.

She observed a squirrel on the tree outside her window. It was perched on a small mid-tree stump which had been cut earlier that year by overzealous pruners. The squirrel was clutching his heart.

Before she stopped to look out the window, June had been reading about a massive trichobezoar. Gastroenterologists removed the giant hairball from a girl on Thanksgiving morning. The hairball weighed ten pounds and was shaped like the stomach in which it had been lodged. The girl had a mental disorder that involved eating her own hair during times of duress. Romantic gastroenterologists called it Rapunzel Syndrome. When asked if the removal of a ten-pound hairball would affect their Thanksgiving meal, the gastroenterologists were quoted as saying, "We don't get fazed by much."

It seemed as if the squirrel was having a seizure. He was shaking, and gripping the tree with three paws. The fourth was still on his chest, as if he was about to break into song. June thought it would be wonderful if the squirrel broke into song. She couldn't take her eyes away, though she was tired, and needed to work and sleep. Helping the squirrel was out of the question, because the tree branch was eight feet from the window. June wasn't sure what she would do to help, anyway. She could do the tiny chest compressions if necessary, but she wouldn't be able to perform mouth-to-mouth resuscitation. She had tried a similar procedure once on a kitten, many years before, and it had not worked.

The hairball girl went to the hospital to have it removed after she lost nearly forty pounds. It turned out that the mass growing in her stomach was filling her up, and though her body begged for protein and energy, everything she ate or drank fell against the knotted hair and clogged in her system. The little food she did eat would eventually break down into enough nutrients to keep her alive long enough to eat more hair.

The squirrel was no longer shaking, June noticed. Its tiny paw still hovered over its breast but the beast simply stared in through the window. June understood dramatics, having recently worked at a dinner theatre, but the performance was a little too compelling. The spirit and knowledge in the eyes was gone, and the squirrel was dead.

Somehow, its tiny claws had dug deep enough into the wet wood—it was raining now, June saw—to keep it righted on the mid-tree stump. The squirrel had honey-brown fur that was the same color as June's hair, still twisting around her finger. June and the squirrel were only two stories up, which still seemed a long way to jump or fall.

That morning, June and her friends had a laugh over breakfast about how they would each die. June had claimed skin cancer, pointing to some questionable moles on her forearms. Another friend swore that after a lifetime of watching his partner smoke, he would be the one with an ironic cancer of the lung. Cancer is funniest when discussed over breakfast.

June tried to see the humor in things. It was a character trait of which she was proud, her ability to laugh at any situation. She joked about love and death. She thought the ball of hair stuck in the girl was hilarious. She often made a joke about the last gift her grandmother sent, a single pair of red socks with a row of embroidered polar bears. She wore the socks, and when anyone remarked on them, she would say, those were the last present my grandmother gave before her passing.

She never would seriously say "passing." Her grandmother hadn't driven in years and likely wouldn't utilize the HOV lane, but June imagined the woman in a dirty red sedan, flipping the bird as she tore around a school bus and howling at the idea that a pair of socks could make so many people feel like shit.

The girl with Rapunzel Syndrome claimed she ate her hair out of heartbreak. June understood heartbreak, having recently worked at a dinner theatre.

The squirrel was dead for sure. It was staring through June with eyes that had seemed glassy before but were practically mirrors at that point. The squirrel swayed along with the tree. Raindrops dripped from its sagging tail.

June smiled at the poor squirrel, wondering about where the rest of it was at that moment. That was funny because she usually saved ridiculous thoughts about the afterlife for animals or people close to her. When the kitten died, for example, June invented the idea that the pitiful creature would return to the world as a ballerina.

She twisted her hair around her finger and watched the squirrel, which had passed. Her knuckle, wound tight with hair, was nearly at her scalp, and her hand was held against her head by her own hair. June wondered if it would be a comfort. She could barely see her own reflection in the windowpane, and when she squinted, it appeared that the squirrel was sitting on her shoulder. June closed her eyes and pulled her hand away in a ripping clump, making a sound like an animal might make. A brown leaf blew against the squirrel, against its face, and then whipped past. June twisted the hair into a knot and swallowed it without chewing.

She was distinctly aware of her body and skin. The squirrel pitched forward with the swaying tree branch. The times, they were changing.

THOUGHTS WHILE STROLLING

Harry Austin Clapp, creator of "Thoughts," a column that ran in this newspaper every week for a score or more years, died at the age of 79, at his home in Collegeport, Saturday, December 25th at 10 o'clock following an illness of several months. Traveller, explorer, engineer, writer, philosopher, real estate man, Harry Austin Clapp rounded out a full and complete life before he passed quietly away.

The Daily Tribune *(Bay City, Matagorda County, Texas)*
December 27, 1937

Recent rain great for crops and makes the figs glisten and show green.

The people of the town have never seen such a warm rain. Fat raindrops make the figs glow, showing the people of the town a new color of green that they've never known before, a green which they call Fig. The townspeople say that this rain is the beginning of things. That year, five families name their first-born sons Fig.

Oscar Chapin growing a ninety-pound watermelon.

Or is the watermelon growing Oscar Chapin? The neighbors begin to wonder. He sits all day by the watermelon, on the ground next to the watermelon in its wooden crate lined with old rags. He takes an eyedropper of water every ten minutes to strategic areas of the ground, under which he says he can feel the root growing. Oscar Chapin claims this watermelon has given him new eyes.

Train crew go to Kingsville with the engine.

Everyone makes a big fuss about it and rightly so, as it takes twenty strong men to lift the train diesel engine into the auto that will transport it to Kingsville. They also travel by train, which makes some of the townspeople think philosophical thoughts about building a train so strong that no train can transport its engine. Likely a train of this nature would need to be constructed in Galveston.

Jim Hale better train his dog.

That dog runs the perimeter of Hale's yard, treading the ground until he makes a ditch. Dog says, "Hey, come over here." When you do, that damn dog gives you a recipe for lemon bars which omits egg yolks and disappoints you sincerely.

Found a dirty face powder puff in my mailbox.

If I were a younger man, I would suspect intrigue from the daughters of the farmer next door. Surely they would have left it as a token from their girl-friend, who felt tender emotions for me. As a younger man, I would contemplate this while holding the dirty face powder puff under my nose and breathing in a heaven's scent of woman's skin. As an old man, I suspect a group of rowdy boys.

Seth Corse suffering from "tizit" in the back.

What happens is this: we tell the young boy, Seth Corse, he has a beetle on his back. The boy turns round and round and says "tizit, tizit?" All in attendance laugh mightily. This is a game we play on Thursdays.

The Come-Inn afloat with water Saturday.

Nothing but trouble for landlord Gus Franzen. Buckets and extra towels were loaned across the land to ease cleanup for the waterlocked sops at the Come-Inn. The building lifted clean off the foundation as if someone cut the concrete with a blade. When Franzen flung open the door in the morning he was greeted by a boy named Fig who was floating on a dinner table.

Freshly graded roads impassable.

Even when you don't walk the full length of a freshly graded road, you must stand at the edge of the work and smell the tar and earth. Half of the crew sickened themselves with drink in Kingsville and did not arrive home in time to operate the static roller, which means the road itself is rough enough to cut the soles of your feet through your shoes if you're foolish enough to walk over it. Passing traffic will compact the road into grooves like a pack of running dogs. I must take a shortcut through the neighbor's pasture.

School board holding a meeting and electing teachers for the next year.

Women are intoxicating and cruel.

Emmitt Chiles is now a member of the ancient order of grandfathers. Came Saturday, and a nine pound boy.

Brought the new family a pan of lemon bars. They observed the strange color and texture of the custard filling and told me Thank you Harry, would you like to see the baby? Humiliation radiated from all in the room. Even the baby felt its first wave of humiliation, spreading across his face like the fever that would eventually claim him. That damn dog.

Worms feedin' on the cotton crop. Time to use a wormacide.

On the back of the wormacide bottle there is one warning: Do not plunge your hands into the dark earth and hold them still until nature renews its movement and you feel the delicate pulse of thousands of worms through your fingertips and across your palms. Such a feeling will make it very difficult to use this wormacide.

By parcel post—twenty-five Jersey Black Giant chicks from Ohio. Arrived one hundred percent.

Open the manila envelope and the chicks come tumbling out, covered in their own excrement and feeling betrayed but alive, cry to the heavens, alive after a long and difficult journey, the world around them tinged with gold. They are granted five hours of freedom before they are locked in the coop out back.

The sun is trying in vain to peep between the heavy clouds.

One understands the feeling, thinking back with some shame to a dress heavy like soaking wet lead, like a velvet bag full of bullets. Everything you touch turns to fire.

Frogs croaking.

Turn them over and tickle them, the young boys say to the girls. After much conversing and screeching, one brave girl picks up a slick frog, green as a fig. She flips it over so delicately in her small palm that the boys stop their shoving and feel strange for watching. The girl extends one slender finger and runs it slowly up and down the frog's exposed belly. When the frog urinates on her, she looks at the boys with loathing. She will later go on to swallow two goldfish alive.

A goose on the slough ranch sounds its rasping call.

The ugliest image in the area. People come from far afield to observe it and feel better about their own lives. On this morning I see a man leaning on his auto, smoking a cigarette and observing the slough ranch goose. The man flicks his cigarette into the wet ditch and drives on.

The something that makes an onion grow; an auto run; a man move and act; a bird sing—where is it generated? Anyone answer?

In the smallest chamber of the heart: Desire.

The mourning dove made her nest in the low tide ground. Foolish bird. Your eggs are now covered with water. The oriole's nest swinging high in a tree is safe and dry.

The foolish oriole, lemon-colored, swings at the wind's mercy and prays for her eggs. It is a wise mourning dove who drowns her eggs before they hatch, for the nature of the mourning dove is to perch on a branch above the low tide ground and grieve the swamp.

The latest fad from Paree is to tie a black silk ribbon around your ankle. For girls only, of course.

A language is born: the manner in which the black silk ribbon is tied determines the personality of the girl who ties it. A half-hitch means she is searching for a kind gentleman to walk her to the market. A sheep-shank means she is a scurrilous woman who wishes to entrap a gentleman with kind words. A figure-of-eight means the time has come for sober discussions regarding the future. The children steal a black silk ribbon and tie it round a frog.

Two and half miles of cement laid on the Collegeport road in less than three weeks is some progress. Thus does our "nine-foot sidewalk" grow.

The sidewalk grows unobserved, save for the men building it. Once it is there, everyone walks on it, assuming it has always been. It has not always been.

Rosalie and her sister buying candy.

Rosalie and her sister enchant all who fall under their gaze. Their pockets are stuffed with peppermint sticks. A flock of orioles groom their brunette hair. Black ribbons tied in timber hitch knots flutter from their ankles. The bloom of youth!

The extra engine crew eating breakfast at the Come-Inn.

The boys are back from Kingsville and tired from the journey but Gus Franzen puts them directly to work, shoring up the building's foundation and repairing the wooden slats around the door. The men blot their faces with rags under the shade tree out back and lay the load of sopping rags in rows to dry. Gus Franzen serves them lemonade and promises to have their rags cleaned before the next dinner service.

Old Sport coming home for an extra meal.

Proprietors of local restaurants wave to him as he walks, saying Hello, Emmitt, care for a drink? A moment off your feet? They know that if they get Old Sport in, they won't have to sell another plate for the rest of the night. He'll eat a porterhouse steak before he sits down. The proprietors claim he eats more than the President, though this claim is unsubstantiated. Today, Old Sport waves them all off. He goes home and sits across the table from his new grandson. Together, they eat creamed peas. These happy days will not last.

Buckshot catching a rabbit.

Naming a dog Buckshot seems a cruel thing, like telling the dog he will never be as effective as his namesake. Such an insult is similar to giving a boy the name of his father.

A mocking bird bringing material for a nest. A little late, but it will soon house four eggs.

A little late, thinks the mocking bird, settling down over her doomed eggs. Her mate brings the sliced-off top of a strawberry for her. He perches on the side of the nest and watches her eat the rare treat. He watches the strawberry, which he still tastes on his beak. He watches the eggs upon which his mate sits. A little late, he says. A little late, she responds. It becomes part of their call to one another: *A-little-late! A-little-late!*

A big crane walking in the slough.

The big crane resolved to kill the goose when he got it alone. He walked the slough for hours, moving slowly from his nest across the field to the spot where the goose would be sounding its rasping call. When he arrives, the big crane sees the goose is not alone. In fact, the goose has an entire audience of pitiable folk. A family with young children watches, mouths agape. Three men stand in a group with their cigarettes. A young woman sits in the passenger seat of an auto, weeping. The big crane, not given to sentimentality, turns and walks home.

A road runner hastening across the new road grade.

A road that slices through shoes leaves no trace on the bird. It is a magical bird on a magical road, the kind of road that chooses its travelers instead of the other way around. This road dreams of becoming less traveled. Orioles flock to the road and line up in rows on either side. They dive after bugs flying off windshields as the autos paint a deep insult of two matching grooved tracks. The road groans and is compressed.

Way off yonder a dog howls.

That damn dog is laughing.

The recent heavy rain insures a good crop so says Gus Franzen.

Gus Franzen stands before his ruined Come-Inn, which inspectors determined was a danger to the public. Workers come from Galveston with notices and boards, stepping over rows of rags. They shutter the place far more efficiently than he ever ran it. Gus Franzen watches them work. After the men are gone, he collects the rags one by one and puts them in a basket.

TRIP ADVISORY: THE BOYHOOD HOME OF FORMER PRESIDENT RONALD REAGAN

Before you visit the Boyhood Home of Former President Ronald Reagan, you should first note that there are, in actuality, *many* Boyhood Homes of Former President Ronald Reagan. Choose wisely and you will find yourself in the fully restored Boyhood Home that served as a Boyhood Home of Former President Ronald Reagan from 1920 to 1923. It is located in Dixon, Illinois, home of the Petunia Festival.

For the purposes of this report, think of the Dixon, Illinois, home—where Former President Ronald Reagan spent the ninth, 10th, 11th, and 12th years of his life: essential, formative years—as the Definitive Boyhood Home of Former President Ronald Reagan and, therefore, as the only Boyhood Home that will be discussed, though he was born above a bakery and surely felt on many occasions the wholesome heat of warm bread.

Very little of the furniture, carpeting, foundation, and artifacts within the Boyhood Home of Former President Ronald Reagan is original to the site. The reason for this is that old things smell terrible.

Within the Boyhood Home of Former President Ronald

Reagan, you will find Former President Ronald Reagan's Fully Restored Boyhood Bedroom, featuring items you might expect a 9-, 10-, 11-, or 12-year-old boy to have owned between the years of 1920 and 1923. These items cycle seasonally within the Home and could include baseball cards, autograph books, footballs, and wooden cup-and-ball toys. While Former President Ronald Reagan never actually touched or considered these actual artifacts, you will be encouraged to observe and consider the objects in terms of their importance to Our Nation's History. Think: Would Former President Ronald Reagan have excelled at cup-and-ball, or would he have swung the toy around by its handle and launched it onto the roof, and how might those actions have later affected his Cold War policy?

The importance of visiting the Boyhood Home of Former President Ronald Reagan to your personal life is clear and unchallenged. Touring the Home will give you a powerful feeling: You will realize that, in fact, we all had Boyhood or Girlhood homes, and that, though none of us are destined for the greatness that awaited 9-year-old Ronald Reagan, we all have a manner of greatness within us, untapped perhaps for many years, but held there in the heart, like a secret.

One part of the Boyhood Home of Former President Ronald Reagan serves as a centerpiece to visitors and Boyhood Home employees: four pennies, hidden in the spaces in the brick wall. Former President Ronald Reagan insisted on replacing the pennies at the final ceremonies for the Restored Boyhood Home, and while he replaced the pennies, he told the lucky crowd in attendance that, as a child, he used to hide money in the bricks of that very wall. Of course, the wall was actually not original, but completely restored, and Former President Ronald Reagan had in fact called ahead to order the workers to leave one brick loose, so that he might tell the story and replace the pennies and please the crowd. The show was always of paramount importance to Former President Ronald Reagan, and, if visitors concentrate, they might be able to picture an 11-year-old Ronald Reagan hiding the pennies in the bricks of the wall and dreaming of the day that he might place different pennies in restored bricks, put there specially for him, so that he might tell the story.

It should be noted that the four pennies in the brick within the Boyhood Home of Former President Ronald Reagan are not the pennies that Ronald Reagan placed within the brick while telling the story at the final ceremonies for the Restored Boyhood Home. The pennies are actually replica pennies, but are within view of the Actual Pennies Former President Ronald Reagan used during the ceremony. The Actual Pennies are of great value and are mounted to a plaque over the mantle. The replica pennies, meanwhile, have their own worth beyond monetary value, for they act as a symbol of a symbol of a very powerful symbol.

Visitors are advised to take care in preparing for the Boyhood Home of Former President Ronald Reagan. All are encouraged to wash their hands before touching doorknobs and rails, to wear shoes with soft soles, and to speak quietly and with reverence. Visitors are reminded to refrain from flash photography, to not carry in food or drink, and to take the time to respect each orderly room of the Boyhood Home of Former President Ronald Reagan, because it is integral to the history of the world, because it is sacred ground.

CODE OF OPERATION: SNAKE FARM

The thing is that everyone is jealous and I hate to say it but everyone is jealous because I am finally creating a SNAKE FARM which has been my lifelong dream, and I spent a very long time in the world saving up for this dream to become a reality as they say on the television *for this dream to become a reality* and at each of the jobs (gas station, collision repair, hardware store) I pinched the pennies and thought about how to create a SNAKE FARM that will really appeal to the masses and I came up with a plan and detailed it in a notebook because I have always been told that *I have fine organizational skills.* The plan is as follows:

Safety First!
The goal of the SNAKE FARM is not only to make lots of $$$ but to show the public once and for all that SNAKES are not FRIGHTENING, many are not even DEADLY but that they are SAFE and often FRIENDLY. It is therefore important that the snakes who are a danger to the community be placed under wire mesh cages and that only *trained professionals such as myself* will handle the snakes. In the occasion that a garter/green snake

seems interested in being touched, children may hold and touch the snakes. Pythons will be touched but not while digesting *because disturbing the lunch of a snake is cruel.*

Care and Comfort!

It should be known that SNAKES are not used to THE GOOD LIFE. They are used to being compared with evil, being that they have no legs, being that they tempted *that woman*, being that they DO have the ability to defend themselves. If visitors only realized that *many of us have the ability to defend ourselves but that we do not advertise this ability with fangs,* they could understand how CLOSE we are to snakes. In the meantime, the habitat of the snakes will be improved with soft dirt, places to shed scales (dark places), fresh food (living) and other surprises that even the snakes could not foresee.

Visiting Hours!

The snakes do not live in a hospital and should therefore not be confined to the hours that a nameless faceless ENTITY has chosen for them. Obviously the snakes cannot talk but their disposition on any given day will determine the SNAKE FARM hours of operation. If for example the snakes are coiled around a tree, the hours will be shortened. If the snakes seem interested in visiting by displaying *tendencies* (sunning themselves on rocks, showing healthy appetite), hours will be extended *until the snakes are tired of this treatment.* The hours of operation will be determined daily via a MAJORITY VOTE among the snakes.

Owner Tours!

As the proprietor of the SNAKE FARM and owner of the land the snakes the cages the information kiosk and the refreshment stand I WILL PERSONALLY give *special behind-the-scenes tours* to all willing to pay a slightly accelerated fee. Visitors paying this fee will have the pleasure of seeing 1) the holding pens and preparation for feeding time, 2) the process of preserving sheddings, and 3) the OWNER'S OFFICE which contains many plans for future expanding, including a small coaster ride for children, coasters being the obvious choice as they are snake-shaped and children riding along them will understand *the serpentine quality of many things.*

Suggested Dress!

All visitors to the SNAKE FARM will be advised to come prepared with the proper clothing which will be: long pants for the men and children, shoes with closed-toes, shirts untucked (important in case of accidental snake release). Long dresses for ladies, to make it difficult for snakes to cling (in case of accidental release). Ladies will be advised to wear a floral print in soft colors, to soothe and comfort the snakes. Fellow visitors and employees of the SNAKE FARM may be *soothed and comforted incidentally* but the snakes in THIS and ALL situations are the #1 PRIORITY.

Research Projects!

The SNAKE FARM will become *a center of research for the county,* drawing students from public schools as well as scholars from the local farm and community colleges. Because of the potential for RESEARCH on interesting and unusual snakes there will be a special day set aside for these students to observe and experiment. Of course the snakes will be cared for and at ANY SIGN OF DISTRESS the experiment will be OVER and the SNAKE FARM will go into LOCKDOWN. To avoid contamination and *maintain a professional atmosphere,* lab coats will be provided.

Feeding Time!

Digestion time is a special personal time for snakes but one of the most fascinating times to observe a snake is during FEEDING TIME directly prior. It should be known that many snakes actually enjoy putting on a show for an audience during this time, much to the dismay of *the animal which will be consumed* but as a capitalistic venture and as a favor to the snakes, FEEDING TIME will be announced and may be observed at the visitor's discretion. It will be advised that children observe, because contrary to popular belief, the mind of a child can take in *much more horror* than that of an adult, that it can be a detriment in fact to deprive a child of the facts of life as they say on television *the facts of life*.

What to Expect!

Visitors to the SNAKE FARM will see snakes in great number and variation. They will see milk snakes and ball pythons and garter snakes, and vipers and rattlesnakes and king snakes and adder snakes and diamondback snakes, and tiger snakes corn snakes cottonmouth snakes asp snakes rat snakes. Many inferior SNAKE FARMS try to keep and show other animals such as turtles alligators bats and baboons but I as owner and proprietor of this SNAKE FARM will insist that there only be snakes. THERE WILL BE ONLY SNAKES.

THE TORTOISE AND THE HARE

When the tortoise walked in, the hare nearly cried out in misery. He had been promised visitors by the night nurse, who was pretty and gave him an extra serving of gelatin when he asked. The hare had made the old mistake and figured that someone so pretty would never give him bad news, but there he was, and here was the tortoise.

"Hello," said the tortoise. A bouquet of wilting lilies was taped to his shell.

"It's good to see you," murmured the hare. Perhaps if he pretended it hurt to open his eyes, the tortoise would leave. The hare squinted and squirmed.

Oblivious, the tortoise attempted to sit in the chair by the bedside. He did this by leaning back, supporting his weight with his hind legs, and then hefting his front legs onto the chair. The chair, on casters, rolled back. The tortoise lumbered to where the chair had rolled and repeated the process again. Finally, he got the chair wedged between the bed and the IV unit. He pitched his body upwards, scrabbling at the upholstery. If the night nurse walked by, she would surely assume the tortoise was attempting to mount the chair. Perhaps she would call security.

The tortoise dug in with his claws, pulled himself into the seat and turned around to face the hare, crushing the flowers taped to his back in the process. His breathing was laborious. "I hear you are dying," the tortoise said.

That's a delicate way to put it, thought the hare. "Indeed I am," he said. "They gave me eight weeks to live a year ago, and I beat the odds."

The tortoise nodded.

Asshole, thought the hare. "I was real outspoken about it for a while," he said. "I got into the paper. The thing was, I was just taking multivitamins and running every day, then I did a whole-body cleanse every two weeks." He stretched his legs and felt the diminished muscle tone.

"The odds caught up," said the tortoise. With his big eyes, he did seem a little doleful. Then again, he always did. He clearly hadn't cleaned his shell before the visit and smelled like a distant scummy pond. Talk about a sanitary environment, the hare thought.

The hare pressed on. "Everybody's got to go sometime," he said. "You'll go. Maybe you'll get the cancer and die next year. I can't imagine you'd have too much trouble succumbing to the odds, as it were. No offense to you, but it takes some serious mental acuity."

"I'm not sure," the tortoise said, "that tortoises can get the cancer." He was trying unsuccessfully to reach around his massive shell to the flowers. He plucked one petal off in his claw and brought it close to his eye, frowning. Perhaps he wanted to eat it.

"Don't worry about the flowers," said the hare. "I saw them when you came in. They were very nice Easter lilies. Daylilies are my favorite but they're a bit rare, a bit hard to find. You might find a daylily in a soup if you look in the right place. You'd have to travel across the ocean but you might just find it in China. Can you imagine it? A flower in a soup. Believe it or not, and I suggest you believe it."

The tortoise sighed. "Friend," he said.

The hare looked at the place where the night nurse had shaved his fur to insert the IV needle. The skin was puckered and red in the shaved place. "I guess you win," the hare said.

"There never was a race," said the tortoise. His shell wobbled a little as he scooted the chair forward and leaned precariously over to touch the hare's paw with the flat portion of his beak. The hare could feel the warm air streaming from the tortoise's nostrils, the cool air rushing in. The hare closed his eyes and pretended to sleep until the tortoise left. He breathed evenly with noise of the machine hooked up to his body. The night nurse came and went. It was a very long wait indeed.

FISH

Dale was married to a paring knife and Howard was married to a bag of frozen tilapia. Each had fallen into their respective arrangements having decided independently that there was no greater match for them in life.

When anyone asked Dale if he had dated actual women before making the decision to marry a paring knife, he would look at that person with such incredulity that the stranger would feel as if they had been rude to inquire. Dale did love his paring knife. They had their problems, like any couple.

Obviously, Howard admitted, a bag of frozen tilapia was different in many ways from a woman, though in many ways it was the same.

***

Howard arrived early to Dale's apartment and found the man finishing breakfast. The paring knife was propped up against a book on the table and Dale's galoshes were next to the door.

"Morning," Dale said. "Coffee?"

Howard accepted a cup and waited at the table. "Warm out," he said. He liked to keep talking to a minimum until they got on the water.

"I know it," Dale said from the other room. "We went on a walk and watched the sun rise across the field. Sweat right through my shirt."

The paring knife was stuck into its usual cork. Howard felt that keeping it out on display was a little silly. When he brought his portable cooler out with him and people asked questions, he said he was a diabetic and needed special medicine. He didn't bother making people understand his personal life. That's why it was called a *personal* life, Howard figured.

Dale emerged from the back room with his baitcaster. "Sorry for the late start," he said, pulling a six-pack of beer from the fridge.

"No problem."

"You make sandwiches?"

"They're in the cooler."

Dale nodded. "I had some problems down at the DMV," he said. "They installed a security checker, and everyone was all up in arms about me bringing in a weapon. I was holding up the line, I had to talk to some supervisor. After all that, I didn't even have the right identification."

Howard grunted.

Dale fit the baitcaster on its rod. "Can't let that kind of treatment go. It's a concept of self-respect. If people can't treat with respect, what are we supposed to do? As a civilization. You know what I'm saying?"

"Sure."

"All I'm asking for is what's fair for me and my family. This country has long flagged on the equal rights front and this is another card in the deck."

"People might think it's strange, is all," Howard said. "It's none of their business."

Dale picked up the paring knife and placed it cork-down in his breast pocket. "It's not their problem," he said. "That's what it is."

"It's not your problem, either," Howard said, picking up the six-pack. "Let's get out there."

***

The two fisherman sat all morning without a single bite. It was a few hours in before they got to talking.

"Explain women," Dale said.

They enjoyed having these theoretical discussions, though they were both married and each secretly felt he understood women well enough.

Howard leaned his shins against the cooler as he spoke. "We're fishermen who don't eat fish," he said. "We catch fish, but we enjoy pointing out interesting things about their fins and scales."

"Remember that trout I caught with the two mouths?"

"That trout was mutated."

"It only ate with one of those mouths," Dale said. "I cut it up later and that second mouth was a vestigial situation."

"That's exactly what I'm saying."

Dale looked out at the quiet pond. He liked to avoid misunderstandings. "We don't eat fish," he said.

"We are interested in fish, but we don't eat fish."

It felt like the kind of morning where men end up making decisions, Dale figured. He was using his old baitcast reel, the Rick Clunn model. He had a lot of respect for Rick Clunn, a professional angler who seemed to keep his life in order with more ease than the average man. He was determined to practice his fan cast that morning, sending the line out like the arm of a clock in an attempt to cover as much water as possible with each cast. The line kept falling slack and Dale eased back into his old overhand. Howard was dozing under his cap, head bowed.

Dale considered Rick Clunn's idea that angling is an art form, and that his own artistic growth faltered until he recognized it as such. Rick Clunn felt that the highest level of his aspiration as an angler was to help a select few touch perfection in that which they most enjoyed. Rick Clunn felt that the world's troubles were caused by everyone else mucking up the works with details and greed.

Dale, for his part, felt that the world's troubles were caused by simple misunderstandings. From sprawling wars to domestic disputes, any problem could be easily drawn down to something happening and a person or group of people getting the wrong idea.

The theory was cemented in his mind every time he brought his paring knife with him to church.

There they were, dressed for service. Every week, Dale pressed his pants and sharpened her blade lovingly against the oilstone. He knew it looked a little strange for a man to prop a paring knife next to him in the pew, he *realized* that, but he figured that as long as he kept the tip of the blade protected with a cork, nobody would say anything. One Sunday, the head usher tapped him on the shoulder as the first hymn began.

"I'm sorry to disturb you," the usher said, once they reached the narthex. They sat on the spare pew under the picture window, as they did when they had these conversations. Dale's paring knife rested between them.

"It's no trouble," Dale said. They were Presbyterians, which meant they were unfailingly polite.

"The knife is bothering folks again," the usher said. "I know you don't mean to."

"Who is bothered?"

AMELIA GRAY

"It's a new family. We're trying to keep them in the flock. We value young families, as you know."

"My wife and I are a young family," Dale said.

"And we welcome and accommodate you, as we have for years."

"I wonder if we would feel more welcome if we had children."

The usher took a long moment to scrape a patch of candle wax from the wooden pew with a credit card. Wax shavings drifted to the seat between them. "Of course that's not necessary," he said. "Perhaps you could keep your wife in your breast pocket? Close to your heart?" The usher nodded politely to the paring knife.

"I respect your position," Dale said. "I respect that we can have a dialogue about this. But when I'm sitting in church, I'm trying to hear a sermon, and everybody else should be too. Instead, everyone's swiveling around and looking at me, and you're having to come drag me out."

"They don't understand your position," the usher said.

"Darn right they don't understand my position. That's exactly what I'm trying to say, here. This is a misunderstanding on their part."

"And in turn, would you say you perhaps misunderstand their position?"

"I don't understand it," Dale said, "but I don't misunderstand it. There's a slight difference there."

"But a difference, all the same."

The sermon was over and the organ had begun to play the offertory. Dale and the usher stood. "I may as well head out and beat the rush," Dale said.

"For what it's worth," the usher said, "I think she's a handsome knife."

Dale slipped her into his breast pocket. "I appreciate that, sir."

**

FISH 71

Howard sometimes wanted to cook and eat the frozen tilapia, but he always resisted. He made a special portable cooler, one that could be plugged into a wall outlet or a cigarette lighter. This allowed Howard to keep the wife in bed with him, even to take her on short trips, such as to the Western history museum Howard loved, the one with the special barbed-wire exhibit. There were many different types of barbed-wire, but his favorite was the type with the independently rotating spurs, five every yard. It was too bad about the safety glass. If the safety glass was not in place, Howard would flick the spurs, sending rust flying. He had fitted his portable cooler with a convenient shoulder strap, which allowed him to carry the wife right into the museum. They could be in there for an hour and a half before thawing became an issue.

By noon, there were a few more boats on the water, and the campers were moving around on the shore. Dale adjusted the rod and watched the patterns his line made on the water. His Rick Clunn baitcaster glinted in the sun. "Here's my thoughts," Dale said. "As adults, we experience a finite number of crystallizing moments in our lives, these points when we each had to close the door on a person or a feeling, or a way of life. The night of that formal dance in high school, I closed the door on women."

It took Howard some energy to consider that far back. "Because Jan Parmentel got sick?"

"She could have at least told her girlfriends to tell me."

Howard reeled in his line and cast it again. "Seems like a minor infraction."

"Sure, it was. It was. But it hit me at just the right time, right on my sweet spot. You know how baseball bats have a sweet spot, and you hit the ball right at that spot and it flies over the fence? Every time?"

AMELIA GRAY

Dale looked to Howard for confirmation. Howard twitched his line.

"Winter Formal 1983 was my sweet spot," Dale said, "and Jan Parmentel was the last girl on Earth."

Howard's portable cooler was empty at his feet, as the bag of frozen tilapia was snug in with sandwiches and beer in their larger cooler. Dale's paring knife was still in his breast pocket. It rubbed a little against the side of the pocket and had begun to slightly cut the fabric. It was just a few threads every day, but soon the shirt would be ruined. On the shore, a lone camper, a woman in a black bathing suit, was waving. They watched her.

"I believe that woman is waving at us," Howard said.

"She's just waving," Dale said. "She's not waving at us."

"It looks like she's by herself out there."

Dale squinted. "You think?"

"Maybe she needs help."

"That isn't our business."

"Come on, now. A woman's out there waving directly at us, and you're saying that's none of our business? There's some idea of implicit blame there, if something was happening to her.

It was difficult to see the woman from where they were sitting, but she was definitely moving her arms in their direction. Howard could barely make out the black of her bathing suit and the white of her legs. She had both hands over her head. Howard reeled in and started the motor. "Let's just have a look," he said.

***

On shore, Wendy finished her beer and backed up to accommodate the advancing boat. "Howdy," she said, snapping the wide band of her bathing suit on an encroaching mosquito. The men stepped out of the boat and pulled it farther ashore. Dale reached in and retrieved his Rick Clunn baitcaster and rod, carefully securing the line.

"Hi there," said Howard.

"Good day for fishing."

"Were you waving at us?" Dale asked.

"Pardon?"

"Settle a bet," he said. "Were you waving?"

"I was stretching," Wendy said. She had a wide smile that displayed the line of gums above her teeth. Howard estimated her to be about five years younger than he.

"Knew it," Dale said. "I knew it."

"We were just getting ready for a little lunch," Howard said. "Mind joining us?"

"Sure, I've got a couple extra beers. I was about to have a bite, myself."

Howard hauled the cooler out of the boat and planted it next to Wendy's lawn chair. "I'm Howard, this is Dale."

"Wendy," she said. She was pretty, Howard observed. They shook hands and she reached into her backpack. "Care for a beer?"

"I've got one right here, thanks." He opened his cooler and pulled the sandwiches out with his beer. The plastic bag holding the sandwiches had opened, and Howard examined the food inside, wrapped with wax paper. The bread was wet but salvageable. He handed the drier sandwich to Dale and picked a soaked piece of bread off a second. They were bologna sandwiches, which reminded Howard of school. He wasn't sure how a plain girl like Jan Parmentel could ruin a man's entire outlook on life

Dale was eating his sandwich and watching them moodily.

"Sorry they're a bit wet," Howard said. "The bag broke."

"It's a good sandwich," Dale said.

"Bologna from the old days."

"What old days?"

"Back in school, like we were talking about."

Dale shook his head. "I didn't eat bologna."

"Sure you did," Howard said. "You loved those sandwiches. You got my mother to pack you an extra one on Fridays."

"I never liked bologna. I never ate it."

They stared at each other. "We appear to be at an impasse," Howard said.

"We can be at whatever you want, Howard. This is the first bologna sandwich I have ever eaten."

"In your life?" Wendy asked.

Dale grinned at her and lifted the sandwich.

"He's full of shit," Howard said.

"Tasty sandwich," Dale said.

Howard closed the lid of the cooler with his foot. "How can you know you never liked bologna if you've never had it?"

"What I meant is, I never liked the idea of it."

"That's *not* what you meant."

"What did I mean?"

"I don't know what you meant." Howard flung a piece of soaked bread into the woods. "What you meant is a mystery between you and Jesus."

Dale took a careful bite of his sandwich. "I'm not sure we have to bring higher powers into it," he said. "I'm just enjoying a sandwich while you enjoy our fine company, here." He smiled at Wendy, who smiled back a little nervously. She leaned towards the cooler and opened it again. "Whatcha got in there?" she asked, and before Howard could stop her, she pulled out the bag of frozen tilapia. "Seems a bit expensive for bait, hmm?"

"Let's have that," Howard said, trying to reach casually for the bag.

Wendy pulled it back, playfully, and turned it over as if examining the package. "Don't these things have mercury in them? That could be bad bait, you know. Can't have a mercury level in your body, that never goes away." She snorted. "Unlike some things."

"S'not bait," Howard said.

"What's that?"

"It's not bait."

"What is it, then? Lunch?" She held the bag with both hands at the corner, as if she was going to open it. She flicked at the plastic with one fingernail, then balanced the whole bag in her open palm as she used the other hand to snap at her bathing suit strap again. She tossed the bag in the air and caught it with one hand. She saw the look on Howard's face and started to laugh, displaying her shining gums. The pillow of white skin across her thighs rippled as she laughed. His expression opened something dark and playful in her, and she laughed louder, holding the bag over her head, dropping it into her lap. Howard stared at her, helpless.

Dale, deciding at that moment that he had seen enough, picked his fishing pole, gripped the rod backwards, and clocked Wendy on the mouth with his Rick Clunn baitcaster. It happened in one smooth movement, almost natural. The anodized aluminum frame of the baitcaster landed with a smart *thwup* on the woman's face.

Wendy howled and fell back, dropping the bag of frozen tilapia and holding her reddening face. "You bastard," she managed, reeling.

Howard scooped up the bag, threw it back in the cooler, hefted the cooler onto the boat, and pushed it off. Dale was right behind him, wading fast through the water in his galoshes. Neither of them looked back. The engine started on the third try, and they were four hundred feet off the shore in half a minute. They could barely hear the woman screaming over the sound of the engine.

Howard couldn't bear to look back. "That was unnecessary," he said.

"She'll be all right."

"We were having a conversation."

"You weren't going to do anything."

"That was god damn unnecessary."

"Are you kidding?" Dale said. "She was about to open it."

Howard reached into the cooler and pulled out the bag of frozen tilapia. Bringing the bag to his mouth, he gripped it with his teeth in the same place where Wendy had held it. He pulled open the bag and flung it, frozen tilapia and all, across the water. Howard spit out the plastic that had lodged between his teeth.

Dale gasped. "What have you done?"

The water was speckled with glittering, frozen white fish fillets. They floated, bobbing with the boat.

"We don't eat fish," Howard said.

They had been too long on the water, and the day of fishing was over. The motor and their commotion scared everything off. Still, the men were slow to leave, watching the tilapia waver uncertainly before sinking. Dale felt like he had been in the sun too long, like he was going to be sick.

When they finally came ashore, and the police were there with that woman, he wasn't immediately sure why. "You've got the wrong idea," he kept saying, "you've got the wrong idea," but explanations vanished. They caught hold of him, and both officers had to wrestle him to the ground to take his knife away.

THERE WILL BE SENSE

And then, though they had a choice, the doctors put a generator in my heart, and they gave me a magnetic band to wear on my wrist which I must pass over my heart when the old feelings begin again. *Arnold*, they say, *you are certainly a special man*. The following are true:

1. Because of a history of powerful migraines accompanied by the trilling melody of seizure, I had certain precautions installed to prevent me from biting off my tongue;

2. A side effect of the migraines is a disorder called Alice in Wonderland which causes worlds to complicate outside of my control;

3. The word "special" often carries both positive and negative connotations.

Jeannie serves me tostadas at the café, the gold cross on her necklace (warm, no doubt, from her skin and the heat of the deep fryer) dangling close to my sweet iced tea. It's the first thing I see as I come out of the dangerous haze, and I feel small and close enough to the cross to make a leap for it. I'd like to dig my finger-nails into the soft cooling gold and balance on the arm of it as on a tree branch, holding the chain for support.

"Watch the plate," Jeannie calls from miles above. She throws herself back like a gymnast and vertigo pins me to the wall. The generator in my heart ticks one sad farewell tick and silences. I miss it already.

"I almost had a seizure," I say.

"I sneak up," she says. She points to her soft-soled shoes. "Sorry if I scared you."

"You didn't," I say. "It was in my head."

Jeannie smiles like an acolyte. "Tostadas are the special today," she says.

"They look special."

"Are you Catholic?" she asks, folding the plate's towel under her arm. There's nobody else in the restaurant except the cook who, finished with the obligation of soaking a corn tortilla in tomato puree and calling it a tostada, is lighting his cigarette on the grill. "I thought I saw you blessing yourself a minute ago," Jeannie says. "I'm just wondering."

"God is very important to me," I say, though what she saw as spiritual devotion was an act that has always been purely physical, my body prompting the machine to prompt my heart to regulate my brain's foolish attempt to revolt against the whole. Religious women are often interested in me because they misinterpret the event. I am often interested in them because they remind me of my mother. This is not strange.

Jeannie rolls silverware and talks to the cook. My tostada depresses me and when I leave, I feel it in my stomach as a whole. My stomach conforms to the shape of the corn discus. I avoid eye contact out of shame.

This town has one fountain, and I pass by it on the walk home. People come to watch the water go up and down, and they throw coins in the fountain and feed the birds around it. It's an idyllic little scene. What the world needs is more fountains. The corn disk is cutting the soft lining of my stomach in half and I lie down on a bench, feeling embarrassed and oppressively blocked. The only other person at the fountain today is a woman wearing a zippered pouch around her waist. She sits with her feet in the water, looking in, and every few minutes she reaches, takes a handful of money, shakes her hand a few times (water's qualities in sunlight: mirrors, jewels, fire) and drops it into the zippered pouch.

"That's illegal," I say.

"I reject law," she says. "This fountain has no laws."

"What about gravity?"

"That's just a good idea."

The tostada grows three times larger in my stomach. I have the brief sensation of the woman shooting far away, into the trees at the edge of the park, me tied to the bench without hope of pursuit. The feeling passes before I think to move my arm.

"That money goes to charity," I say.

"What do I look like?" the woman says.

I tilt my head to look up at her. She's wearing blue linen pants, wet at the calves from the fountain, and a white shirt. Her hair is tied up with a yellow kerchief, which has the effect of pulling her features up and back, lengthening her neck, brightening her face. I feel heat like a rash. "The Virgin Mary," I say.

"The Virgin Mary?" she says. "That's strange."

"No, it's not."

She stands up. Her zippered pouch drips water down her leg. She is unusually tall.

I have to shut my eyes. "I'm sorry," I say. "I'm disoriented."

"Story of my life," she says. When I open my eyes, she's vaulting over a line of bushes on the other side of the park. I think, good. The world needs tougher religious artifacts. Everything you find on Sunday morning is too delicate. Candles burning over white linen. Transferring the wine from vessel to vessel, chasuble sleeves hanging perilously close. You can buy all this stuff from a catalog, but it's expensive. Sometimes, it comes blessed.

The fountain is very close to my home and at my home's heart is my medicine cabinet. Something feels very strange about the container of my body. As I was getting up, the corn disk hardened into a circular saw blade and went to work on the flesh of my organs. It consumes and spins faster and threatens my spinal cord. My brain howls in protest. I want darkness and my bed and the calming mechanism of a great deal of medication.

My brain says, *careful what you wish for!*

The next day, Jeannie serves me King Ranch chicken at the café. She has her hair pulled back.

"Your hair looks nice like that," I say.

"I wear it like this every day," she says. This sounds a little accusatory and I feel like apologizing for not noticing and then I resent the desire to apologize for not noticing because it's not as if noticing her is my responsibility. I have lately been thinking about responsibility. The chicken is congealed to my plate under a solid grease-mound of cheese.

"What are your responsibilities?" I ask Jeannie.

She glances at her other table, two women who are also having the King Ranch chicken. It is the special. "I take orders," she says, looking back. "And I bring out water and I serve plates and some-times I say 'that plate is hot.' I roll silverware, I cut lemons and limes, I clean the women's restroom and I wash the windows and I change the specials board and write receipts and make change."

"That sounds like a great deal of responsibility," I say, thinking of lists—1. bring out water 2. serve plates 2a. that plate is hot 2b. I hope you enjoy the food 3. roll silverware 3a. this silverware is heavy and right 3b. what am I going to do about my problems 4. cut 4a. lemons 4b. limes 5. clean 5a. windows 5b. restroom 5c. specials board—"but I meant in your whole life."

"That's a lot more," she says, smiling.

"I imagine so."

She picks up my menu. "What are your responsibilities?"

"To keep my body alive, and my mind well."

"That's it?" she says. "Well, you're lucky."

I cut through cold cheese with the side of my fork. "I am the luckiest man alive," I say. "I am the luckiest man in the history of the free world."

"Don't you have a job, though? Don't you have any goals?"

These questions make me uncomfortable. There is a poster behind her of peppers from around the world and I wonder which pepper would be the worst on the tongue. Then, if you swallowed them, which pepper would be the worst in the gut, and how would the burn differ. Jeannie would not be interested in me if I told her that I got checks from my mother and from the government and, though I respect the necessary existence of each, that I dislike both as sources of revenue, and that my goal is her, or someone like her. These are normal ways to think but no way to talk to a religious woman.

"My goals are to be alive and well," I say, "and to be closer to God."

"Those are good goals."

"I want to get so close to God that God has to file a restraining order."

QUESTIONS FROM THE FLOOR

Q: Why does Jeannie like you?

A: Jeannie appreciates my honesty and understands that there is not nearly enough of it in men in the world these days. She has not given it much thought.

Q: Is it possible that she will break your heart?
A: She would need a much larger magnet.

Q: Do you expect us to believe you?
A: You have absolutely no choice.

Q: We resent this, Arnold. Please give us a reason to trust you.
A: The reason is that you have absolutely no choice.

Q: Don't you feel that God is *so beyond* caring what is going on down here?
A:

The fountain is broken. The water in the concrete basin is still, and the pumps are shut off. A man in work clothes is bent over an electrical box I never noticed, twisting wires. I think of the electrical box in my chest and feel a little sorry for myself.

"The water is powered by electricity," I say to the man. "Doesn't that seem like a cop-out?"

The man pulls a crimping tool out of his box. "I'd be out of a job if it wasn't," he says.

"What are your responsibilities?"

"To keep food on the table," he says, turning his attention to the electrical box.

"You're lucky you don't live on a boat."

"What's that?"

"You're lucky you don't live on a boat on the ocean. It would make things difficult."

"Fishermen make a lot of money these days," the man says. "I was watching a show about it. It's profitable but dangerous."

We live in a world where fishing is sexy. "My responsibilities are to keep my body alive, and my mind well," I call out to the man working in the electrical box.

"That's hard to do on your own," the man says. He's hiding in his work clothes. All I see is blue denim and brown belt. This man is a novice practitioner of the electrical box and is growing smaller by the second. This is terrifying to me and I call out, "I'm doing the best I can!"

I'm very worried that the man will become the electrical box and that the fountain will never be repaired. "Please be careful!" I yell desperately towards the smooth denim, a hanging curtain now, over the electrical box. My hand comes up, my wrist, and I start the generator in my chest. The battery is tiny and creates a small alien warmth as I am brought back hard to the world.

From my brain, an urgent message:

Why did you do that? We were all about to have a good time. If it weren't for you and your precious medical science, we'd be orbiting Saturn right now and watching the stars fall. You call this keeping your mind well? We're all well on our way to crushing boredom, that's all. But don't worry about us. It's not as if we power your dirty shell through this world. It's not as if we spend all day waiting for a nap in the sun, only to find you jogging us back to your own pointless day-to-day. We have nothing better to do. Please, continue.

My brain is diseased with logic.

Jeannie tells me that the daily specials in the café are always the food they didn't sell enough of from the day before. She points at my sloppy joe.

"Taco meat from Thursday and marinara sauce. Some ketchup."

"What about the King Ranch?"

"Chicken quesadillas. The tortillas went stale."

"How late do you work tonight?"

She looks at me and doesn't say anything. Under the table, I rip my napkin in half, and then in half again, and again and it's snowing white paper over my shoes.

"You might want to come to my home for dinner," I say.

When Jeannie and I walk to my home, the following does not happen.

1. We turn miniscule but not unimportant, and find that blades of grass have their own weapons, though they are weapons against small insects, who look like demons at close proximity;

2. The sidewalk turns liquid and claims us, drawing us deep through hot sharp earth, where we meet those from generations past as well as some people working in a coal mine;

3. A wise man confronts us and suggests that the *Pieta* is the most beautiful piece of art ever made by a human in the history of the world and while I don't disagree I think it might be even better as a fountain.

I do, however, realize that Jeannie is essential to not one but both of my responsibilities and is therefore very precious to me. She nourishes my body with her daily leftover specials and she is strong and essential to the health and safety of my mind. It is when I look dreamily at the pendular motion of her golden cross that I realize I feel entirely well. Inside my heart, the generator rides the thumping aortic valve in blissful, silent contentment. Jeannie's hair flows behind her like a river. I am in ecstasy.

In my home, Jeannie looks around. "It's cleaner than I thought," she says.

I offer her a mint because I'm not sure what else to do with her. We are both very shy, and we are not used to interpersonal communication outside the arena of the café. I do feel very shy. My generator feels that I feel very shy.

She pinches a mint with clean fingers. We both smell like ground beef.

"Where did you get this box?" she says.

"From a catalog."

"It's adorable," she says, taking it and turning it over in her hands. "Isn't this what priests keep communion wafers in?"

"A pyx," I say. "It came blessed."

She looks around the room. Her eyes see: table, books, parament, pyx collection, stove, palm fronds, window, stained glass. In the stained glass, she sees tiny bubbles which contain worlds.

"Did all this come from a catalog?" she says.

"The oven came with the apartment."

She laughs, and then she stops laughing. She looks at the oven and I want to tell her that it actually did come with the apartment and that's not a joke and she's really quite kind to come over for dinner and I'm sorry that I didn't make anything and moreover that I don't have anything in the house to eat because I usually take my meals out because it's good for the spirit and as usual what's good for the spirit is bad for the wallet.

Jeannie sits down at the table and begins to cry. I touch her hair with my lips and her head is warm and smells like a glass of milk. She sobs and holds her fists closed on her knees.

"I'm sorry," she says. "I'm frightened."

My fingertips brush against the place where her hair is drawn up in a ponytail and I say, "you certainly shouldn't be frightened of me, if that is what you are frightened of."

"No," she says. "I am having a fight with my husband and I have nobody to talk about it with. I am frightened he will leave me," she says.

(*Then, a terrible thing happens: My brain leaves the picture entirely. The room goes completely black, and the spotlight comes up on the two of us—Jeannie at the table, with my brainless body propped up behind her. Someone coughs. The curtain man lights his cigarette and digs into the fuse box.)*

JEANNIE
(in tears)
I am frightened he will leave me.

ARNOLD
Don't be frightened. Please, let's talk about it, between the two of us. Let's work out a solution for you.

JEANNIE
I can't do that. I feel awful about doing this to you, burdening you with this.

ARNOLD
(putting his hands on her shoulders)
It's no trouble at all, my dear. Can't you see? I care very much for you. How long have you been married?

JEANNIE
Six months. He's a good man, he has a good job. He's great in bed—

ARNOLD
And why don't you wear a ring?

JEANNIE
We're getting rings tattooed on our fingers as soon as we can find the perfect artist. I figure it's more lasting that way.

ARNOLD
So what's the problem?

JEANNIE
If you'd let me get to it—

ARNOLD
(laughs suddenly)
I just don't see the problem then, pretty girl like you, a
newlywed, striking out in the world with a sensitive and
handsome man—

JEANNIE
Whoever said he was handsome?

ARNOLD
Your responsibility overall is to care for your own life and your
own handsome husband because he is a lucky man and to see you
sad should be one of the great sadnesses in his life and I'll tell you
that honestly, it should be one of his greatest sadnesses.

JEANNIE
Whoever said he was handsome?

BLACKOUT.

"What gives?"
"Sorry." I reach for the wall, feeling for the switch. When I find
it, she's looking at me with fish eyes.
"I think I'd better go," she says. She stands up and I shrink
back in my chair. "But thank you for the advice."

She is a tower of a woman! In the center of my seat, I am acutely aware of the false-feeling velvet under my hands.

"Would you like a glass of water?" I ask the tower of Jeannie.

"No, thank you." She reaches across the room and puts her hand on the doorknob. She fills my apartment and I cower in the low cover of the chair cushion. And then the *whump whump* of my brain as it comes down the stairs two at a time, looking for breakfast. As she leaves, she sees a man alone at his kitchen table, blessing himself before the invisible feast.

After that, as after all great tragedies, the days go by:

Jeannie serves me meatloaf at the café.

Jeannie serves me spaghetti and meatballs at the café.

Jeannie serves me pork barbecue and french fries at the café.

Jeannie serves me breakfast tacos at the café.

Jeannie serves me fajitas at the café.

Jeannie serves me onion soup at the café.

Jeannie serves me quesadillas at the café.

Jeannie serves me chicken fried steak at the café.

Jeannie serves me grilled cheese sandwiches at the café.

Jeannie serves me steak and eggs at the café.

Jeannie serves me baked potato at the café.

Jeannie serves me tomato soup at the café.

Jeannie serves me pork chops at the café.

Jeannie serves me cheese crisp at the café.

Jeannie serves me ham and cheese at the café.

Jeannie serves me fish sandwiches at the café.

Jeannie serves me chicken salad at the café.

Jeannie serves me corn dogs at the café.

Jeannie serves me tamale pie at the café.

Jeannie serves me vegetable soup at the café.

Jeannie serves me macaroni at the café.

Jeannie serves me chili at the café.

And one day, I come home to find the Virgin Mary sitting at my kitchen table.

"Hey there," she says. She is eating mints from my favorite pyx.

"How did you get in here?"

"I try doors. Aren't you that guy from the fountain?" She offers me a mint.

My hands are huge and I am concerned they will flatten her in the course of my reach. She watches my awkward progress with careful pinhole eyes. When I touch the pyx, she snaps it closed.

"What is life?" she asks.

"Alive," I say, "and well."

She nods once, grandly. "I thought you might know, if anybody did."

DIARY OF THE BLOCKAGE

DAY 1

I am hesitant to talk about it, but I'm the kind of person who turns off the television when the newscaster starts in on colon cancer. Therefore, I must say this delicately: it so happened that I came down with a mild stomach virus, hopefully gone by the morning but tonight was difficult and in the course of my time in the restroom I succeeded in expelling most of my dinner save for one small and stubborn piece which managed to lodge, it seems, between my esophagus and windpipe. At three in the morning I was crouched in bed and swallowing chronically, painfully aware of the foreign mass that will not move up or down but only vibrates unpleasantly. In the morning, I will call the doctor.

DAY 2

I did not call the doctor. I went so far as to find my insurance card, but I could imagine the *remember Miss Mosely, well she has had a thing lodged in her throat* all within range of anyone with half a mind to be within earshot of the office window. I feel very sincerely that bodily functions have their place, but why would the toiletries and makeup and personal privacy industries all be such multimillion dollar successes if the place for those bodily functions was in public? To say otherwise is to disrespect culture. Meanwhile, the object makes itself known whenever I swallow or cough but is otherwise not troublesome. I can't decide if it is disintegrating or I am growing used to it. I think it is a piece of hamburger.

DAY 3

It is not disintegrating. It is much like a jilted lover: when it heard its presence in the world was becoming bearable, it revealed itself to be living down the street, to frequent the same local eateries and second-hand stores once enjoyed on peaceful solitary afternoons. I have changed my diet. I avoided hot coffee with my breakfast though it left me useless and squinting at the turn arrow against the sun. I brought a tomato from home for lunch because the thought of my usual hamburger out was distinctly unpalatable, but I realized too late that the acid of the tomato plus the salt I sprinkled on it (the only way to reasonably enjoy a tomato) stung my throat and left me pitiful and nearly in tears, crouched in my cubicle. I have begun meditating. I can picture the fleshy walls of my delicate throat, red and raw, with the blockage the size of a small fingernail touching two sides of the void, vibrating with my vocal cords when I speak and avoiding, by some cosmic misfortune, the tomato and milk and corn chips and yogurt I send to destroy it.

DAY 4

Office meeting today. Mr. Wallace brought in hot coffee and orange juice. During the meeting I discovered I can widen and collapse my palate around the blockage. It requires a slight back and forth motion of the head (imagine a small bird) and dominated my efforts over talk of redistricting, distribution, advertising, human resources news, 401-K plan changes. I picked out of obligation the orange juice believing it to be the lesser of liquid evils but of course it goes down like murder. I consider the possibility of a very successful diet: allow yourself to chew and enjoy the taste and texture of many foods, but at the point of swallowing, simply spit out the morsel and replace it with a healthier alternative such as a vitamin pill. In my case, something easier on the throat-parts such as ice water. I wish to patent this diet and to advertise its concepts in small checkout counter books across the country.

DAY 5

Worrisome creaking sounds and feelings from the throat. I feel a moment of judgment or shame: the reason for my stomach flu of Saturday night was perhaps exacerbated by the drinks I had out at what I surmised to be a singles' bar, drinks that would have been far less troubling to my long-term health had I not seen my first husband, who suggested with his own meaty-fisted drink that I had not yet had enough and who am I to deny a challenge! (The blockage encourages me to feel this way.) I can admit that yes, the confrontation may have been a part of it. I sit on my couch and cough for a satisfying amount of time before falling asleep to the sounds of smooth jazz.

DAY 6

When I recall my behavior from that first night (there was a throwing of drinks and some shouting), I repeat a litany of self-assurances. I am kind, I am thoughtful and beautiful, I am clever, I am kind I am thoughtful and beautiful I am kind of clever and thoughtful and beautiful and kind though clever. I must perform the litany in a somewhat secret manner. I have taken to ducking my head under my desk as if I am looking for a dropped pencil and then I can begin my meditations. The blockage seems to grow—tinier pieces of food and digestive acid and saliva perhaps. When I cough or swallow, the vibrations seem lower and longer, more permanent. I don't mind adding to it. Strange, how the disgusting becomes commonplace and then welcome. I wonder how long I would have to live with a parasite, a tapeworm or a leech, before it became a happy addition to the host of my body. I look at myself in mirrors obsessively.

AMELIA GRAY

DAY 7

Power outage due to hail storm. I wonder, has anyone created a candle wax remover with an attachment that allows the remover to make new candles? A kind of catch system with a heated core. The resultant recycled candle would be multicolored from the different waxes and in that way it would be wholly the property of the consumer and free of obligation to a consumer system. I have many good ideas. I find that when I lie down, I have consistent trouble breathing. Swallowing also grows more painful. I force down some of the cottage cheese otherwise curdling in the warming refrigerator. Through this pain I have decided I must learn a valuable lesson. In the night's uncomfortable darkness, I consider my connection to the past and future of the planet. I take off my arch support shoes and remove my under-eye coverup gel when I undress for bed. I am quietly aware of my flat feet. Propped up on pillows, I touch the lump swelling gently on my throat.

DAY 8

A cloud to every silver lining! I have finally begun to internalize the blockage—it feels strange even to write "blockage," because I forget what exactly it was blocking and why I felt so constrained. I found the plunging neckline shirts in the back of my closet and wore one out to lunch. I allowed the stares and gestures towards me with cool disregard. I sat at a table in the center of the room. For lunch? Ice water, ice water, ice water! Later, I drink a protein shake out of desperation and collapse on the kitchen floor, sobbing.

DAY 9

My delicate condition has brought me a kind of daily transcendence as I move through the world. The girl who argues politics in front of the coffee shop has gaps under her fake nails where the real ones are growing, and she's waiting for the problem to get obvious enough to do something about it. The young man who listens to her has a piece of hair that never lies down flat. He is very disturbed by this and will lick his fingers and slick it down when he thinks nobody else is watching. I am very interested in necks, and how their owners handle them. People mostly ignore their own necks, except for very nervous girls who hold them while they talk as if they are trying to keep their vocal chords from exploding and splattering across the other person.

DAY 10

I have a very interesting theory in terms of my condition: I am fairly sure that it never existed—never in any real, physical form. Can I conjure a physical event out of darkness? Could I imagine my toenails shorter? Could I create, using my mind, an object that has never existed before, anywhere in the world? *Is such a material, at this very moment, within my throat?* Tenderly, I carry within me the first invented treasure known to mankind. My body is the first supernatural wonder of the world. I am careful when I cough, afraid of disturbing the gestation period, protective of the mass.

DAY 11

I have considered feeding myself intravenously but I worry that medical professionals would realize the unique quality of the blockage, and would conspire to take it from me.

DAY 12

Mr. Wallace called today to ask why I haven't been coming to work. I had been a model employee in terms of attendance and grooming. I wish I could press the appropriate button and confirm that *yes*, I was feeling fine, that *yes*, I would like to keep my job, that *it would be nice* if everyone understood that I was doing something for the *benefit of the world* and that my duties as a paper-mover would have to wait. The colors in my body have moved and centralized at my throat. There is a terrible pallor in my face and hands but I am heartened by the growing darkness around the strange, wonderful object.

DAY 13

The swirling patterns behind my eyes confirm what I have secretly felt for days, that it is time for the blockage to finally emerge, the gestation period has concluded, the suffering is nearly through (though it has not been true suffering and we will never know true suffering), that which will most closely resemble joy is prepared to leave my body and move into the world!

DAY 14

I am wildly aware of the feel of everyday things. My body feels wholly perishable against the tile and dirt and ground it touches. I set out the silver bowl I once received as a wedding present (so long ago, such strange emotions!) as well as a set of silver spoons and monogrammed hand towels. My plan was to expel the Object into the bowl, but when I attempted the expellation (hunched over the bowl on the floor, which I chose to be the easiest method for both myself and the Object) I was greeted by a sharp, shocking pain. My nose bled into the bowl and I hunched nearly blind with emotion but the blockage screamed *OUT* and my grasping hands touched bowl, towel and finally spoons! And gratefully I took a spoon in my shaking grip and fully formed ideas flashed before me, Stop the bleeding! Save the Object! And I do understand that this will be a difficult labor, indeed!

THE CUBE

The children who found the cube shrieked over it as children do. The adults couldn't be pulled away from the picnic at first, and assumed that the children had found a shedded snakeskin or a gopher hole. Only when the Rogers kid touched the iron cube and burned his hand did the parents come running, attracted by the screams.

It was a massive monolith, wider than it was tall and taller than anyone could reach, wavering like an oasis in the heat. The Rogers kid wept bitterly, his hand already swelling with a blister.

Nobody knew what to make of the thing. It was too big to have been carted in on a pickup truck. It would be too large for the open bed of an eighteen-wheeler, and even then there were no tire marks in the area, no damaged vegetation and not even a road nearby wide enough for a load that size. It was as if the block had been cast in its spot and destined to remain. And then there was the issue of the inscription.

They didn't notice it at first, between the screaming Rogers kid, his mother's wailing panic to hustle him back to camp for ice, and the pandemonium of parents finding their own children and clasping them to their chests and lifting them up at once. The object in question itself received little scrutiny. Only when the mothers walked their children back to camp for calamine lotion and jelly beans did the rest of the adults notice the printed text, sized no larger than a half inch, on the shady side of the block:

EVERYTHING MUST EVENTUALLY SINK.

The words caused an uncomfortable stir among the gathered crowd.

"What about Noah's Ark?" asked one man in the silence.

"After the flood, the ark was lost in the sand."

"What about buoys?"

"Given time and water retention," said a woman who worked in a laboratory, "a buoy will sink like the rest."

This was disconcerting news. Everyone stood around a while, thinking.

"What about an indestructable balloon?"

"Such a contraption does not exist, and is therefore not a thing."

"A floating bird, such as a swan?"

"It will die and then sink," the first man said, annoyed.

One man made to rest against the iron cube and stepped back, grimacing in pain at the surface heat.

"A glass bubble, then."

The laboratory woman shook her head. "The glass would eventually erode, as would polymer, plastic, wood, and ceramic. We are talking thousands of years, but of course it would happen."

The group was becoming visibly nervous. One young man recalled a flood in his hometown that brought all the watertight caskets bobbing out of the earth, rising triumphantly out of the water like breeching whales. The water eventually found its way though the leak-proof seals and the caskets sank again.

Another man recalled a mother from the city who drove her car into a pond, her children still strapped to their seats.

A man and a woman walked to camp and returned shortly with a cooler of beer. The gathered crowd commenced to drinking, forming a half-circle around the cube. They agreed that many things would eventually sink:

> A credit card
> A potato (peeled)
> A baby stroller
> A canoe
> A pickle jar full of helium
> A rattan deck chair
> A mattress made of NASA foam

They even agreed on alternate theories: everything that sunk could rise again, for example. One of the men splashed a few ounces of beer on the iron surface as a gesture of respect. The place where the beer touched cooled down and the man leaned on the cube. It didn't budge.

The men and women grew drunk and their claims more grandiose (a skyscraper, an orchard, a city of mermaids). Eventually, the mothers came to lead them back to camp but they didn't want to go, eliciting words from the mothers, who had been stuck with the children and each other all afternoon and were ready for the silence of their respective cars. Back at camp, they were throwing leftover food into the pond. Ducks paddled up to eat the bread crumbs and slices of meat and the children clapped. The Rogers kid stayed on his mother's lap, picking jelly beans from her hand.

A pair of siblings threw an entire loaf of bread into the water and watched it disappear.

The mothers didn't talk much, preoccupied with children or ducks. As they sat, some thought about the children, and some thought about everything eventually sinking, but most thought of the long drive ahead, the end of the weekend, and the days after that.

LOVE, MORTAR

My love for you is like a brick. It sits silent in me when you bring out
my food at the Dine and Dart, red tray aloft, your skin gleaming
like grilled onions. My love is rough around the edges but solid
through the center, fresh from the kiln. My love for you is heavy
and dark, Jenny, it builds and breaks down, Jenny, it cracks the
windows between you and me—you, mixing milkshakes for little
league winners, and me, miserly with sandwich wrappers in my
car. You, smiling down at the register like a woman with secrets,
and me, in agony over the golden arch of your eyebrow.

A brick, inert and dangerous. This love can be worn down but
there is always substance to it, always heft, as when you struggle
to lift the box of flash-frozen patties, that iced meat against your
bare arms, the cold thickness of your flesh a barrier against the
protected warmth of your lungs, your heart, your bones. When
your manager helps you with that box, the brick grinds in my
chest. Your manager, Bill of the blue eyes, Bill of the "no parking"
policy, Bill of the fast-food tie. He tucks it in his shirt as he walks
to the bathroom. You might be kind and claim that Bill is a good
man but what you'll soon learn is that there are no good men,

Jenny, none left at all. Not even me, though I'm good deep down, almost to the center.

Almost to the center. But the center of me is that brick. It's there when you bring my cheeseburger no lettuce on a steaming red tray. It's there when you reach into your flat front pouch for my straw. It's there when you pull your hair up behind your visor when you go in for your shift and when you lean over the grease trap with your scraper and bucket. It's there when you stand at the register, Jenny, your unpainted fingernails hovering over the keys as you think of those old dollar bills, the tens and rolls of quarters, wondering if you shouldn't just no-sale the register and open it, one of those times when blue-eyed striped tie Bill is smoking a cigarette in the bathroom and looking at the Sears catalog he has hidden behind the toilet. You could just open that register and reach in with two hands and pull out fistfuls of cash and put it into your front pocket, stuffing it all down there, paper-wrapped straws scattering across the greasy floor. You'd walk out and throw your visor into the garbage and you would never come back.

But where would you go, with your great treasure? I see you on the beach at Galveston, peeling off that thick dirty uniform and walking slow into the water, trading the salt of french fries and tater tots for the healing salt of the ocean. I see you saving souls in that warm water, Jenny, I see you taking men in that water and making bricks of them all. You sink them there and build a wall with them, and create purpose to their roughness and use to their weight. You build a sea wall and stand on the other side with your feet planted wide on the hot sand, your golden hair streaming behind you like a flag of independence.

You have a power, and there is no reason this power should frighten you. Surely you see how Bill looks at you, and the men paving the road and even me over my cheeseburger no lettuce sucking chocolate milk through a straw. We are all drawn to you, but I am the only one who understands that draw, knowing how I started the kiln's fire myself, long ago. Now, my guts are full of clay and you can dig it out yourself. Open me up and hold the dangerous brick in your hands, feel that awful weight.

THIS QUIET COMPLEX

Maria Telesco
Leasing Office
Windy Pointe Apartments
1220 Thorpe Ln.
San Marcos, TX 78666

January 8

Dear Miss Telesco,

As you well know, I typically prefer to address my complaints to you personally. I look forward to the hours we spend together each week, discussing the maintenance terms of my lease. We are women of respect and empathy, and informal communication is often sufficient. However, I felt that I should address my complaint with you today in the form of a signed letter.

I always look forward to the Windy Pointe Apartments' Annual Christmas Decoration Contest. You could say it is one of the few reasons I might remain in an apartment complex with a mold infestation. Thank you, by the way, for sending Charles and Marcus to repaint my ceiling. (They told me it was dust but we both know that's not true, don't we?)

Creating the beauty of the season is a matter of placing clean, bright lights precisely in place, lining the window with washable fire-resistant faux-nettles, and hanging germ-free antimicrobial cloth garland over the balcony in a way that perfectly accents the blue in the rails. Charles was a dear for sanding them, by the way. I know he did not find any termites but it's possible the termites escaped, isn't it? Perhaps the entire rail should be replaced?

Besides the cheer these decorations bring to the hearts of the children of this apartment complex, I have always appreciated the eighty-dollar rent deduction the first place prize always brought. Last year, I used the extra money to purchase a tarpaulin for my living room floor—a once-over with bleach kills the bacteria that falls from the ceiling while I am sleeping at night. This year has been tough, and I was hoping to be able to afford another set of acid-free storage bags for my summer clothes.

Obviously, you cannot imagine my shock and disappointment when Sandra McCloskey in Apartment 3-B won first prize.

Sandra McCloskey placed a tree on her balcony, a real tree that affects my real pine allergies. She "decorated" the tree with strings of popcorn, which attract birds that sit on her unwashed balcony ledge—birds that proceed to defecate, I can only assume, on her balcony rail. Additionally, Sandra McCloskey (I think we can speculate that she is not a Christian woman) invested in one-hundred blue icicle lights, which she did not consider cleaning before nailing them at unevenly spaced intervals to her overhang. I saw her take those lights directly from the box and hang them. I watched her do this.

Miss Telesco, this loss is not a matter of pride for me—at this point, it is a matter of my health and safety. Though my contest entry perfectly blended the purity of artistic expression with the sanctity of an antimicrobial environment, I can understand your position as impartial judge, perhaps wishing to reach out to the younger, pine-loving crowd that has so recently flooded into our quiet home. However, I think it would not be beyond your power to ask Sandra McCloskey to remove her "decorations" at the earliest possible convenience. She's had her fun, she's won her prize. Let her spend the money on tainted meat and ineffective coconut-scented soaps. All I ask is that, in future competitions, you not allow her menace to continue before the eyes of the world, and of God.

Happy New Year!
Helen Sands

VULTURES

The vultures were everywhere. On the local news, the meteorologist speculated calmly after his seven-day forecast that the vultures were eating moss by the river. They weighed down trees and circled over the town.

I found Brenda looking at the sky when I came back from hauling boxes to the trash bins behind the daycare.

"They're over the baseball diamond behind the high school," she said, "three blocks away." She shielded her eyes against the sun, watching.

"Everybody's looking up these days," I said.

"The radio says it's good for the muscles in your neck," Brenda said. Inside, the children had already begun to destroy the carton of Easter eggs we had hidden in the snack room.

***

At home, I told my boyfriend Toby that he had to come with me to Evelyn Merkel's to mop her floors and fight the vultures.

"I don't want to go anywhere near any vultures," he said.

"It's my money, then."

"It would be your money, anyway. I've got some ideas," he said. "I need time to put something together and I can't waste it on vultures."

"Fine," I said.

***

Evelyn Merkel was wearing a housecoat with a nightgown underneath, and her hair was curled in rings that fell over her shoulders. She set her thin hand on Toby's back and gave him a little push over the threshold.

"Out back," she said.

Mrs. Merkel had a metal pole in the yard to hold up the clothesline and two vultures were chasing each other around it. They screeched and darted, beaks terrifying and open, showing sharp tongues. I couldn't figure if they were playing or fighting. When Toby moved the curtains to the side, they turned at once and screamed at us. Mrs. Merkel tugged the curtain back over the window.

"I don't want them knowing we're in here," she said. "Do you two want breakfast?"

"We already ate," I said.

"What do you have?" said Toby.

She had English muffins and unsalted butter. Mrs. Merkel said she wanted to make orange juice but couldn't due to the vultures monopolizing her citrus tree. Out back, the birds made frantic scraping noises against the metal pole.

Toby found a rake in the garage while I finished the dishes. Mrs. Merkel switched on a soap story. Toby stood at the door, gripping the rake with both hands. It was the old kind of rake, with a heavy metal bar at the end and tines that could aerate a lawn if you dragged it. On the television, strangers danced at a party.

"Don't slam the door," Mrs. Merkel said. "Don't kill them."

He laid his palm on the door. "These vultures are symbols," he said.

"Wave that rake around and make some screech noises," she said. "I don't want you killing anything."

One vulture was rooting around in the compost pile, and the other snapped at the clothesline and fell back.

"They're big," Toby said. He slid the door open.

Outside he danced around the vultures with his back to the wall. They shrieked and he swung the rake low to the ground, catching a long divot of grass and flinging it back to the door. Mrs. Merkel turned up the volume on the television and Toby took another swing, passing closer. The birds fell back in unison and took off running, rising. He leaned the rake against the wall and opened the glass door so violently that it smacked into the other side.

"For goodness sake," Mrs. Merkel said.

***

Brenda invited me out to lunches on weekends because she wanted to be my friend. We drank ice water and watched the sky.

"Do you think there are more?" she asked. She wore a thin neck brace almost covered by her turtleneck. "There are more than last week."

"Mrs. Merkel has three more," I said, squeezing lemon over ice, licking my fingers.

"The parents are asking me about it, I don't know what to tell them. They don't think it's safe to bring their children outside."

"Did you tell them it was safe?"

"I don't know if it's safe. I don't think it is." She held her hand to her throat and leaned back in her chair to look up at the sky. "On the radio they say the vultures won't go until they've exhausted a population."

"I just wish somebody would do something about it," she said. "I'd swear that they're after us."

The next morning, I touched Toby's hand. He looked up from the paper. "Mrs. Merkel's vultures are back," I said.

He chewed at the inside of his mouth.

"I can't spend all my time there," I said. "I have a job."

"I can't go. I'm working on an idea." He closed the paper and pushed a yellow pad towards me. On it was a drawing of a refrigerator door, with knobs and buttons in a row across the top.

"What is it?"

"Condiment dispenser. I'm working on the cleaning mechanism, and then I'm going to call a phone number and they're going to start making it."

"Would it really work?" I leaned over to the notepad again and he covered it with his hand.

"You're always talking about how you can't find the right jar of mustard," he said. "This way, they'd all be in a row. There's a panel across the top, you don't even have to open the refrigerator door."

"Do I need to do the rake trick myself?"

"You'd never have to look for mustard again," he said.

***

I showed up thinking Mrs. Merkel wouldn't be home, but when I went to take the sheets off the bed, I found her crouched in the corner of her bedroom.

"I know what they're here for," she said. "They're waiting for me." She had a cardboard box taped over the window.

"They've been circling for days," she said. "They're waiting for me to die."

"Don't say that."

"That's what they do, isn't it? They wait for things to die, and nobody's doing anything to help me." She stared at her cardboard window. "I'm hungry."

The adhesive remover would be in the garage. "I'll make some soup if you come out of here," I said.

Twenty minutes later, she emerged from the bedroom looking apologetic. "I've been alone for fifteen years," she said.

"Your soup is at the table."

She sat down at the table. "I know what they're here for," she said to the soup.

***

When I got home I found Toby on the couch, eating peanuts and drinking champagne from the bottle.

"She's losing it," I said.

"I think we could really do something with this town if we set our minds to it." He passed the bag of peanuts. "I was just thinking, everyone's scared to death of these vultures." He took a drink of champagne and wiped his mouth with the back of his hand. "We need to make some kind of repellant."

I sat at the other end of the couch and he moved his feet to give me more room. "How would we do it?" I asked.

"We play off people's security," he said. "Take a guy afraid they'll find him while he's playing golf. Sell him a golf umbrella with metallic panels."

"Blind the birds?"

"Or a lady who's scared they'll eat her garden. Sell her a bag of quicklime, but you've got 'Vulture Repellant' written real big across the front." He took a long drink of the champagne. "The overhead is practically zero."

Brenda ushered the children inside as soon as they stepped out of their parents' cars. She held them close to her, casting furtive glances at the sky. The children usually played out front on nice afternoons, but the meteorologist's article in the newspaper said the vultures came in with the warm front and to be cautious when allowing children and small animals out.

"Did they carry off Mrs. Merkel's laundry?" Brenda asked. We were eating a snack with the kids.

"She hasn't hung her clothes out in a month. She wears her housecoat and the underwear she put in storage years ago."

"Who puts underwear in storage?"

An animal cracker fell in my glass of milk.

The children had all the typical meaningless adorable things to say. Louis asked if the devil sent the vultures, probably because he had seen the flock circling over the abandoned Methodist church. Brenda's child said the vultures came from the desert and smoked cigarettes.

For the craft project, I came up with the idea of making vulture pictures out of feathers and macaroni. After they finished we could paste on some paragraph printed from a book about where vultures come from, and the kids could take the pictures home to their parents. Brenda put Robert in time-out when he made a picture of a vulture eating his baby brother.

"I don't think I want children," I told Brenda, who was busy separating feathers globbed together with dirty paste.

"They're not bad when you have one at a time," she said.

"You shouldn't wait until you're thirty, though," Brenda said. "Your kid'll end up retarded."

"Where'd you hear that?"

"Radio," she said, sneaking another cracker from the bin. "It's medical science. How are your boyfriend's ideas coming?"

"He's making a vulture repellant."

She finished her cracker and started filling juice cups on a tray.

"That's a pretty good idea," she said. "That's good, that he's trying to do something."

"He wants to poison them."

"He could market that." She drank a cup of juice and filled it again for the tray. "You've got to believe in him, or he's going to lose faith in himself."

"But he wants to kill them."

"I'm not saying you need a man right now, but that man of yours, he's fine. He's no bastard, like Brittney's father. He's an inventor, he's one of those genius types that we don't understand right away." She pursed her lips and picked up the juice tray. "Just let him crack his eggs, honey."

***

The blue panel with yellow flecks I saw in Mrs. Merkel's backyard was, on closer inspection, an image of the Virgin Mary printed cheaply on a hook-stitched rug. It hung from the clothesline. Inside, Mrs. Merkel had meatloaf in the oven.

"Your beau brought it over," she said. "He put the clothesline back up and said a prayer and, wouldn't you know, those buzzards haven't touched the ground since."

We watched Mary from the kitchen window. She held her palm serenely against the possibility of vultures. The blue tassels at the edges of the rug flicked around in the wind. Toby had arranged pillar candles and small statues. The pillar candles had blue and green wax and depicted the Stations of the Cross, and a big white one was set in the center for the resurrection.

"It was so kind," Mrs. Merkel said. "He wants me to call him if they come back down. I'm making meatloaf."

She was wearing an faded yellow dress with a wide, white belt. Her hair was out of curlers and she had it pulled back. She was stirring a pitcher of Tang. "I feel like a million bucks," she said.

"It's not very Methodist, is it?"

She tapped the spoon on the pitcher. "It's more Methodist than shooting them, which is what Mr. Dobbs was doing."

***

Toby was smiling in his sleep. He had my satin eye pillow strapped to his face. I crawled into bed and lay my arm over him, kissing the back of his neck. When the sun came in through the windows and it got too warm, I pointed the fan towards the bed.

On the kitchen table was Toby's stack of receipts, for groceries mostly. On the top was one from the Christian Supply. It was deducted from his total debt, refigured and circled, "$1,103.38," in red pen.

Brenda ordered a crab cake at lunch. "How's the inventor?" she asked.

"He's still working on it."

"Any day now," she said. "You stick with a man like that, he'll hit on something soon enough."

"I'm starting to wonder how long I have to stick, is all."

Brenda's crab cake arrived and she stabbed at it with her fork. "Brit had to go to the vet," she said. "I mean, the doctor. The cat had to go to the vet."

"What's wrong with Brittney?"

"She stuck a ball of paper in her ear. I don't know why she did that. They had to use long tweezers, actually. Cost me twenty dollars."

My chicken salad came in a lump on lettuce leaves. "Why did you have a baby so young, anyway?"

Brenda speared the crab cake and lifted up the corner of it, turning the piece over with her fork.

"Were you scared of the retardation thing?" I asked.

"Yes," she said. She took a bite.

"What's wrong with the cat?" I asked.

"Put it to sleep," she said.

***

The meteorologist interrupted his weekend forecast. "It's a dark world out there," he said, tapping the sensor in his hand and changing the seven-day on the green screen to a picture of a vulture. "We've had a lot of calls and letters." The picture faded and changed to one of a group of vultures closing in on a family. "Keep walking when you leave your house, don't stop for anything. Carry your children and keep your pets on a short leash. Protect your backyard by putting up a chicken wire net."

Brenda stayed five hours past close, hanging a plastic net over the daycare's backyard. She tried to crimp the wires with her hands and ended up in the clinic for tetanus shots. After that, she refused to leave her bed until the vultures left. I had to lead classes. We fingerpainted vultures and made vulture sculptures with popsicle sticks. We drew plans in crayon detailing how to safely trap and release vultures. Robert drew his baby brother as bait. After show-and-tell, I told a story about vultures.

***

Once upon a time, there was a kind princess who lived in a castle protected with spiked walls and lava moats and knights. She had a beautiful garden and a stable full of prize horses but she could never leave the castle because of the killer birds circling day and night. They avoided the spiked walls and flew over the lava moat to stay warm. The knights couldn't reach them with their swords and the situation grew desperate until one of the knights had the brilliant idea to kill one of the smaller horses and fill it with quicklime. The vultures swooped down, gorged themselves and fell dead, and the knights had the whole mess cleaned up before the princess came out for her evening walk.

***

Toby bought fifty golf umbrellas from a wholesaler for his vulture project. He handed me the recalculated debt when I walked in the door.

"I wanted panels of aluminum and fabric glue," he said, "but it was impossible to cut the panels correctly. I ended up buying jumbo rolls of aluminum foil and stapling them to the nylon. That's itemized on the second receipt."

"The second receipt."

"Under the first one. These will sell," he said. A single prototype lay finished between us. "My old manager at the range said he was very interested, and all I showed him was the model." He pointed at the mess of foil and fabric. The staples had snagged on the support poles and ripped the fabric, and he had lined the exposed rips with tape and rows of staples and more foil.

I didn't even want to touch it. "Perhaps the model would benefit from another layer of nylon?"

"I'm doing this for us," he said, carefully examining his work.

"I don't need any help. Thank you, though. I would prefer to do this one for us." He opened the umbrella, and closed it again to keep the top layers of foil intact.

"You could have bought a reflective nylon. Something that wouldn't split so easily."

"You're profiting from this," he said. "I was different before, but I'm helping us now. I'm using my intelligence, and I'm really starting something for us. Don't shut me down already, when you haven't even seen what I can do."

"Listen," I said. "I want to forgive your debt."

Toby picked up his box of forty-nine compact golf umbrellas, his jumbo roll of aluminum foil, both staplers and three cans of spray adhesive, and walked out.

After he left, I turned on the television. The news had a camera following the meteorologist, who made a camouflage tent and camped among the nests in protest of the hunters. The Methodists were holding nightly prayer meetings and when the TV cameras arrived, they played an electric guitar. At the corner store, the shelves of bread and milk were cleaned out. The hunters were taking practice aim at the magpies in the parking lot. The meteorologist took over the camera and was speaking urgently about buckshot and environmental activism. I didn't answer the phone when it rang and Mrs. Merkel cried from the machine that the vultures had gathered on her clothesline and weighed it down towards the candles. Her Virgin Mary rug had been burning for hours.

"Nothing can be done," she cried.

I turned up the volume on the TV, thinking *that rug must look like a miracle.*

THE PIT

EXT. A GRAVEL PIT - DAY

The sun rises over what looks to be a gravel quarry. The bleak land-scape stretches as far as the eye can see, dotted occasionally by a few wandering people dressed in slightly mussed business attire.

> NARRATOR (V.O.)
> In the near future, increasing global
> tensions sparked a war among
> nations spanning years. The
> worldwide destruction multiplied,
> spreading until the world and most
> of its inhabitants were
> annihilated, ground into dust by a
> faceless war machine.

Close in on two men, DAVE and SAM, standing in the gravel pit. They appear to be disheveled but healthy. In different circum-stances, it would look like they were waiting for a bus.

NARRATOR (V.O.) (CONT'D)
Years passed. Those that survived
had to be strong of heart and mind,
tougher than the friends and
neighbors they left gasping in the
dust. These brave men and women
found a way to survive against all
odds and emerged as the unlikely
authors of their own existence.

The men fidget, bored. DAVE checks his watch, examines it,
flicks at it.

NARRATOR (V.O.) (CONT'D)
Years and years passed. With the
threat of global-nuclear conflict
gone, life regained a sense of
normalcy, of peace. The very life
which had always been so difficult
became commonplace.

DAVE
Damn.

SAM
Hmm?

DAVE
My watch broke.

He presents it to SAM, who leans over to examine.

SAM
Bummer.

DAVE
I had that watch for years. Found
it on a guy.

SAM
Nice watch.

DAVE
Dead guy.

SAM
That a Rolex?

DAVE
You know, that's what I thought,
but I don't think it is.

SAM
Did the guy seem like the kind of
guy that would wear a Rolex?

DAVE
He was wearing a suit, you know,
nice suit. Too small. But it was a
nice suit, looked authentic.

SAM
Maybe it was a Rolex.

DAVE

I know suits better than watches,
and all I know about this watch is
it crapped out on me. Supposed to
be one of those self-winding
things.

SAM

Probably got sand in it.

DAVE

I don't even remember what it's
like to not have sand in a thing.
Sand everywhere.

SAM

Everywhere. Hey, is that Linda?

DAVE

Where?

SAM

(*pointing*)

Just over the horizon.

A figure approaches from far away. It is impossible at first to see if
the figure is a man or a woman.

SAM (CONT'D)

Looks like she's headed towards us.

DAVE
I haven't seen Linda in weeks. She
never comes around here. Are you
sure that's her?

The men watch the figure make slow progress towards them.

SAM
No.

DAVE
Yes, it is her.

SAM
I'm not sure.

DAVE
Man, it has been forever since
we've seen Linda. Remember hooking
up with her during that year-long
sex orgy?

SAM
Yes. Yes I do.

DAVE
Crazy times.

SAM
Guess so.

DAVE
Linda. She was a fox and a half,
man. She found that hairbrush, and
she would brush everyone's hair.
Everyone just sitting around in a
circle, remember? She'd circle
around and brush everybody's hair.

SAM
I remember.

DAVE
She's headed this way. That is
definitely Linda.

The figure, LINDA, grows larger, waves.

SAM
I am in love with Linda.

DAVE turns to SAM, surprised.

DAVE
No you're not, Sam.

SAM
Yes I am. I am in love with Linda
and I want to marry her. Is that
what people do when they're in
love?

DAVE
Yeah, I think so.

SAM
Then that's what I want to do.

DAVE
Dude, we haven't seen Linda in a
year and a half. I haven't seen her
since the sex orgy thing. Oh man,
is that weird now, that I was in a
sex orgy with Linda, and you're in
love with her?

SAM
Yeah, that's kind of weird.

DAVE
Man, I'm sorry. I had no idea you
were in love with her. You know I
wouldn't have done that if I had any
idea.

SAM
That's fine. Let's maybe just not
mention it.

The two watch LINDA approach.

DAVE
Linda, huh.

SAM
Linda.

DAVE
Good old Linda. Pretty girl.

SAM
Yes.

DAVE
You have no idea what you're
talking about. You don't know who
this person is.

SAM
What? Of course I do.

DAVE
You are shitting me. You are full
of shit. I can't believe how much
shit can be inside one man. This is
the first woman we see in weeks and
all of a sudden you're in love with
her? I don't think so. No, I know
what's going on here.

SAM
What are you talking about?

LINDA steps into the scene, startling them both.

LINDA
Hi, guys.

DAVE
Hi, Linda.

LINDA
Dave, right?

DAVE
Yeah, hey, you remembered!

LINDA
I never forget. How have you been?

DAVE
Oh, you know. I live in a pit.

All three laugh, and stop laughing. LINDA turns to SAM.

LINDA
And you must be—

SAM
I'm Sam.

LINDA
Have we met?

SAM
Yeah. I think so.

DAVE
You don't remember Sam?

LINDA
(drawing a blank)
Sure I do, I remember Sam. From,
uh, the sex orgy?

SAM
Yes. From that.

LINDA
Crazy times. There had to have been
a hundred fifty people there. Now
that was a party.

SAM
Certainly it was.

LINDA
Now Dave, I remember you from that.
You had these pasties on, right?

DAVE
I forgot all about those!

LINDA
That was hilarious. You kept
swinging them around and around—

LINDA does an impression of the man wearing pasties.

DAVE laughs and joins in.

DAVE
Hey everybody, look what I
can do!

LINDA
Wasn't all you could do, as I
recall.

DAVE
Oh, you.

LINDA
That's all I'm saying.

They smile at each other. SAM's presence becomes conspicuous.

LINDA (CONT'D)
How's tricks, Sam? Still doing your
thing?

SAM
For sure. Yeah.

LINDA
So, guys. I've been walking for
days.

DAVE
Yeah, what's it like over there?

LINDA
What, back there? More of the same.
Really it's just a big gravel pit
as far as the eye can see. Pretty
depressing. I feel like I'm going
insane, you know? Really, truly
insane, for the last time. I
thought I'd pass the time by
chewing all the skin off my arm, right?

DAVE
Gross.

LINDA
Well, yeah. I mean, it grew back, see?

She displays her arm. The men jump back but then lean in,
examining.

DAVE
Oh yeah, that's not bad.

LINDA
Your friend doesn't say much, does he?

DAVE
He's a thoughtful kind of guy.

LINDA
Oh yeah?

DAVE
Sure. You'd really like him if you
got to know him.

LINDA
I usually don't go for the strong,
silent type, so much.

DAVE
He looks strong?

SAM
I'm right here, guys.

LINDA
Looks like a nice guy, though. You
look like a nice man, Sam.

SAM
Thanks, Linda.

LINDA
Play it again, Sam!

SAM
Right.

LINDA
You ever hear that?

SAM
Maybe once.

LINDA
I always loved that movie.
Casablanca.

SAM
Hmm.

LINDA
They were so in love.

SAM
That's actually a misquotation.

LINDA
What? No it's not.

SAM
It is. A common misquotation, you
know. Bogart says, "Play it once,
Sam, for old times' sake."

DAVE
Come on.

LINDA
Sure, but later—

SAM
Later, he says: "Play it, Sam. Play
'As Time Goes By.'" That's what he
says later.

LINDA
(impatient)
But after that.

SAM is getting worked up, a function of a bad Bogart
impression mixed with heartbreak.

SAM
"You played it for her and you can
play it for me!"

LINDA
Are we talking about the same
movie?

DAVE
I'm not sure.

SAM
"If she can stand it, I can! Play it!"

LINDA is clearly disturbed.

DAVE
Sam, I think that's enough.

SAM
(stricken)
Play it!!

LINDA
(to DAVE)
It's all right.
I didn't know anyone cared that
much about one little quotation.

SAM
I've heard it a lot, is all.

LINDA
I hadn't even seen that movie since
the war, you know?

DAVE
It was a great movie.

LINDA
Yeah. Listen, I should go.

This statement takes a moment to sink in —
leaving means walking many days without direction in a gravel
pit.

SAM
Don't go, Linda. I was just having
a little fun.

DAVE
Come on. You just got here.

LINDA
No, it's okay. I have this
appointment in a couple weeks. I
should really start heading in that
direction.

SAM
(desperate)
Linda, I'm sorry.

LINDA
Don't be sorry. I'm sorry.

DAVE
I am also sorry.

LINDA
We are all sorry, then.

She regards the two men with disappointment before turning
and walking in the direction from which she came. They watch
her go. After a minute, DAVE turns to look at SAM, his
expression unclear.

THE END

THE PICTURE WINDOW

There once was a woman who lived on the far edge of town, where the houses had courtyards and vegetable gardens. The woman grew a small amount of flowers and vegetables in her garden, a small plot behind her house. The picture window in her bedroom faced the garden, and she spent many happy weekend hours watching the scene.

One day, she turned away from the window and noticed that the rest of her room looked darker than usual. She assumed that her eyes had gotten too used to the brightness of the window but the room grew darker and darker by the hour and finally vanished into blackness. The window, however, was bright with sunshine and color. She looked out at the beautiful garden for a long while, frightened to look away, and when she finally did look away again she was confronted with total darkness, and she cried and touched the walls and found her telephone and called her doctor.

The woman's doctor and his colleagues were entirely baffled. They traveled to the woman's house, tested her sight, and found it to be entirely disintegrated. At the window, she seemed to recognize the plants and flowers by general color and shape, but when one of the doctors stood in the garden, waving to her through the open space, she continued describing geraniums and the leafy tops of the carrots as if they were all she saw.

Baffled, the doctors stood in the kitchen and discussed the ethics of their situation. It was only right to tell her the truth: the tests on her corneas and pupils had revealed no reaction, and it was total blindness. They were drinking coffee, which they had made for themselves. Certainly, the doctors reasoned, they would tell her to be prepared for the worst while they did some final tests.

When they told the woman that her selective blindness was focused on her window, and perhaps the condition was permanent, the woman looked out the memory of her window and nodded, though she didn't entirely understand. Sunlight filtered in through the tall trees and lit the grass and the garden in shades of green and brown. Soft breezes rustled the leaves and gave her a comforting sense of the wide, changing world. The doctors quietly washed their coffee cups and left them to dry next to the sink.

The woman passed many satisfactory days at her picture window. When she opened her eyes in the morning, she was always briefly afraid of the darkness, but out of the corner of her eye she was comforted by the sight of the glowing window. She stumbled and touched the walls and found her shower, and then dressed herself for the day and dug in her pantry for breakfast. In those first days, she was ashamed to call her friends, so instead she worked through the canned foods in the pantry for basic sustenance. She spooned up pieces of tuna while watching the wind work through the leaves of her summer squash. She tried to go outside, was disturbed by the blindness that remained, and headed back inside.

The woman was suspicious of the idea of selective blindness.

AMELIA GRAY

The doctors asked how her garden looked when they called. She stopped asking about the test results and they did not offer them. She sat in front of the window and held her hand in front of her face. All she saw was the garden. She was a smart woman but the blindness made her desperate, and she convinced herself that the selectivity of her condition actually blocked out anything but pure beauty, and that was why she couldn't see her shower curtain or her stove or even her own body, but still saw so vividly the outside world from inside.

And then, because it eventually had to happen, word got around town. It was only a matter of time before the woman's home became somewhat of a local attraction. A steady stream of students and church groups and retired folks and scientists and psychics and skeptics passed through her doors. Her friends joked that she should take admission, and eventually set up a donation box by the door. They requested any amount for the upkeep of the house as well as care for the poor woman, which they had all partially assumed. The woman woke in the morning to gentle knocking at her bedroom door and sometimes fell asleep at the window and had to be moved into bed by her devoted friends and visitors.

As one grows used to anything, the woman grew used to her visitors. They were friendly, after all, and brought gifts, and told her news from the town and the world beyond, and listened with great interest to events of the garden only she could see. Skeptics sometimes tried to convince her that her vision was false, that there were clouds where she saw solid blue sky, that many of the plants she was describing had in fact died long before and had been replaced with flowers or trees planted by other visitors. The skeptics were hauled out and denied reentry, and the woman was reassured by those who remained that everything she saw was real. A theory had begun to circulate among the believers that the woman's vision of the garden was the true vision, and what they all suffered to see approached the ideal but would never reach it.

The woman's vision never faded. On the day she died, she described caterpillars ascending the vines on the far wall and sunning themselves on wide leaves. After her death, the townspeople made plaques and intricate pieces of art in the woman's honor and created a holiday within the town wherein everyone was required to look very closely at something and to discover something new about it. In this way, they turned the woman's vision and eventually the woman herself into an idea, and their own ideas became much easier to believe.

THE VANISHED

The man had always aspired to live his life as inoffensively as possible, and when his woman came home one evening and found he was gone, she was sure for days that he was around there somewhere. Perhaps he had gone to the bathroom and was in there, quietly creaking, making silent curses over the pipes. Maybe he was in the attic. Or maybe he was working late, something he did not treasure but did with a kind of silent pride that suited him and had always bothered her.

After a few days, it became apparent that the man was not in the backyard or behind the television. She grew nervous, imagining how disappointed he might be upon returning to find that she had not kept the house clean. Indeed, she had forgotten she was in a house at all, and had scattered newspaper across the bedrooms and allowed branches to crowd the door. A thin skin of dust covered the bookshelves and countertops and toaster oven and toilet tank, her desk and his desk. It piled up like snowdrifts in the framed pictures on the wall. She tossed and turned in the bed until the covers parted and formed a protective whorl around her body.

The woman stopped leaving the house. She decided that if her man peeked through the window or knocked lightly on the door and realized that she had gone, he would leave for good. She ate all the fresh food in the house, and then all the canned food, and then the expired food, and then the spices. She washed table-spoons of cinnamon down with tap water. She reached out the windows, pulled leaves from the trees and ate them with the last of the salad dressing. She released the cats so that she would not eat them, and then she ate their food.

The man's father called to ask if there had been any updates, and to inform her that he had called the police. At the time of his call, the woman had been using a dainty flathead screwdriver to open the man's computer. She had wanted to see if the man had left any clues in there, but there was only more dust. She swallowed the computer's tiny screws.

It became apparent that the man had not taken any of his clothes with him. The woman knew that her man owned 3 black undershirts and 5 white, 7 pairs of jeans and 27 button-down shirts, 5 collared polo shirts, 4 t-shirts with silkscreened graphics and one novelty shirt that he only wore as a joke, a button-down two sizes too large and covered in neon images of ice cream and hot dogs. She could not bear to eat it but took it out of the closet and observed it every morning, salivating.

She ate all the pages out of his books.

When the detectives arrived, she apologized for her appearance. She explained that she was too worried to leave the house. She showed them the man's clothes and his personal effects. She took them on a tour of the home and showed them the toilet he used and the ironing board and the grill. The things were untouched, she noted, she had left them untouched. When the man came home, he would appreciate his things being untouched. He was very particular and appreciated her respect and in exchange, he showed her respect. The detectives looked at her distended belly and asked if she was pregnant. She cradled the mass and said that she was.

Things started arriving in the mail. There were bills and notices that the woman no longer understood. It seemed like someone was asking the man to pay a huge sum of money to a credit card and a house. She took all the paper money she had not yet boiled and stuffed it into the envelopes provided and sent them back.

Other letters were more troubling. There was a handwritten letter from the man's grandmother that didn't make any sense until the woman cut out all the words and rearranged it:

TAKE WITH YOU ALL TIME TO WEATHER EXCELLENT PARTS. HELLO WORK TOGETHER UNTIL YOU UNDERSTAND WHAT YOUR FATHER TELL. LOVE YOUR WIFE THEN RETIREMENT. WARM DAYS FORGET NIGHTS. DON'T NEGLECT ENJOY MONDAY.

The woman thought that was all pretty good advice, and taped it to the refrigerator. She opened the refrigerator and ate the baking soda from its box with a spoon.

Some days later, the man's phone rang. He had left it plugged in when he vanished but his woman had not heard it ring before. When she heard it, she vomited into a small trash bin next to the phone. She could barely summon the strength to pull herself up to look at the phone. She couldn't make out the number displayed through the layer of dust. The phone's ring sounded like the old rotary phone her parents kept in their home. She wondered if it was the man calling his own phone, and why that would be. Perhaps she had gotten phones switched and was confused. The phone stopped ringing. The woman placed the phone in her lap, pried the number 2 from the keypad with a screwdriver, and ate it.

It was a terrible idea to go outside again. The woman had seen a couple out the front window and was sure that the man had placed them there for her to see. She banged her fists on the windows to try to get their attention but when they didn't make a move to acknowledge her, she threw open the locks on the door and rushed out.

The couple was a boy and girl couple, and they were eating love right out in the open. They swallowed great handfuls of love, sticky tangled masses of it, standing nose to nose with one another. They were gorging on the stuff. Love dripped from their hands and landed in spatters on their shoes. The boy wiped his hand in his hair and left a long slick. These gluttons of love spread it across each other's mouths. They made wet noises as they consumed.

The woman rushed up to the people and slapped the love out of their hands and said Don't eat that! That's poison! and the boy laughed but the girl looked at her unkindly and bent down to gather the ruined pile of love up from the ground. The woman watched the remainder seep across the asphalt.

Get a hold of yourself, the girl said. The girl clasped the slop to her chest. It bled through her shirt to her skin. Look at what you did, the girl said. The woman looked. She felt relieved, but of course it was not enough.

THE SUITCASE

After a few weeks, Claire noticed that Alex's suitcase was gathering dust. Dirt and cat hair lay piled up against it. "Today's the day you put the suitcase away," she told him.

"What if I have to go on a trip?" he said.

"You haven't touched that suitcase in two years," she said. "You're not going on a trip. You're staying right here, forever."

He leapt out of bed. "Christ's sake. Don't say things like that."

"But we've built a life together."

"Not that part. The other part." He nudged the suitcase with his toe. "This part."

"They call this a fear of commitment."

"I'm not afraid," he said, lifting the zip-up lid of the suitcase. He stepped inside and sat down. "It's you who is afraid. You are the one who is afraid."

Alex curled up in the center of the suitcase. It was a large rolling bag and there was just enough room for him. He reached over to the top flap and pulled it onto himself. Claire peeked over the edge of the bed and only saw a suitcase, closed, the dust disturbed around it. The light bulb in the bedside table lamp popped and went dark.

"I'm staying here," he said. And he did.

***

It was embarrassing to go to the airport with him. The baggage counter women curled their lips at her when she hefted the bag onto the scale. "This bag weighs one hundred eighty-seven pounds," one counter woman said. "There's an extra weight charge. Are you carrying explosives, weapons, or perishable materials?"

"My boyfriend is in there," Claire said, sighing. The x-ray would have caught him, anyway. She was trying to bring him with her to visit her mother in Fort Lauderdale. The counter women called security, who arrived with a luggage cart. They hid their faces behind clipboards and laughed. It was humiliating. They escorted Claire and her bag to the airport chapel, where they were welcomed by a man named Ted who wore a preacher's collar.

"I will lay hands on this bag," said Ted, once security had explained the situation.

"It's really all right," said Claire. She sat down in a chair next to the door. She was happy that she had not been arrested.

Ted lay hands on the bag. It was an olive-colored Samsonite. His hands looked pink against it.

"The devil out of this luggage," he said.

"Piece of shit," Alex said from inside.

Ted crouched to unzip the bag, but Claire put her hand on his arm. Alex had prepared her for just such a situation. "We would rather you didn't," she said.

"They would have needed him to remove his shoes," Ted said.

"Already taken care of," Alex said.

Ted looked at Claire.

"He's nude in there," she said.

"I see," said Ted. He ushered security out of the prayer room and returned with two paper cups of orange juice. "Interesting," he said, handing her one.

The airport chapel was less of an event than she would have figured. The two rooms were softly lit and tiny like a closet. There were thin, colorful pillows on the floor, and five chairs, and a lamp with a stained-glass pattern on the shade. On one wall was a sticky note with the word "MECCA" written in blue marker. On the other wall, Ted leaned and sipped his juice. It was strange to see a man standing up.

"You insisted on traveling with him," Ted said.

Alex jabbed at the side of his bag. "Screw you!"

"Shut up," Claire said, kicking the place where Alex had jabbed. She felt her foot make contact and Alex went silent. She sipped orange juice and watched the bag. "I wanted to bring him to meet my mother. She won't be around much longer and I felt it was important," she said. "Even if it meant her seeing Alex going through this phase."

"I'm not rightly sure how you see this as a phase," Ted said. "That kind of verbiage always strikes me as somewhat armchair-prophet, wouldn't you say?"

Claire regarded the bag, which was already beginning to stir again as Alex regained his bearings. "Of course it's a phase," she said. "We'll come out of it together. I can't have a man fathering children when he won't even leave his luggage."

"How does he live?" Ted asked. "How does he feed himself, or use the restroom? Doesn't he develop terrible sores? What of his work towards his Spirit?"

The Samsonite hopped a little with rage. "We manage, guy," Alex said from within.

"It's time to go home," Claire said.

Ted stood up with her. "I worry," he said. "He's exceeding the weight limit on that luggage." Ted slipped Claire a lined notecard cut down to business card size, his name written on it in marker. Ted closed her hand around the card. "Heaven be with you," he said.

It was dark by the time they got home. Claire unpacked her own suitcase, a small carry-on barely large enough to hold her clothes. She had rolled Alex back to his place at the foot of the bed. "You're too heavy," she said, as she laid him down.

"What a day," he said. "I'll be honest with you. I didn't really want to meet your mother." Alex tended to be more candid since he had gotten into the suitcase.

"I figured."

"Had to do it sometime though, babe. You're real important to me."

Claire ran her index finger down the handle of the suitcase. "I know it," she said.

The porch light went dark with a mighty pop that sounded like a kid had shot it with a pellet gun. She thought herself a relatively self-sufficient woman, all things concerned, but she hadn't yet mustered the organizational skills required to change a light bulb.

"The light," she said. "I'll pick another up from the store tomorrow."

"Plus two sixty-watt candelabra bulbs for the foyer," Ted said. He knew everything about lights. "Plus, three mini halogens for the dining room."

"Candelabra."

"A hundred-watt halogen for the kitchen."

She rested the sole of her bare foot on the suitcase. "One hundred watts," she said.

***

Ted's apartment was well-appointed with items from around the world. He told Claire they were gifts from people visiting the chapel. The most extravagant gifts usually came from some poor guy's family members after Ted administered last rites. People had heart attacks on airplanes all the time, apparently. Ted offered Claire a whiskey with two healthy ice cubes. It was barely noon but she accepted it.

"I didn't know priests were allowed to drink," she said.

Ted raised his own glass. "Wouldn't know either way," he said. "I'm not ordained."

"But you gave last rites? That seems illegal."

"I'm not sure about discussing legalities with a woman who tried to smuggle a man through security."

"He insisted."

"And where is he now?" Ted asked. "Hopefully you didn't leave him in the car."

Claire swirled her drink. "He likes to stay home. Anyway, he didn't like you very much."

"Does he ever come out of the luggage?"

"He sticks his legs out to stretch them sometimes," she said. "He likes to avoid cramping his legs."

"Well then, perhaps he is just a man after all."

"I know he is a man."

"You haven't touched your drink." Ted had mastered the sustained eye contact of the overtly religious.

"I hadn't thought about it."

"Well then, perhaps you are just a woman."

"Really," Claire said. "Maybe you are on to something."

He watched her like a dog watches the door. She stared at him until he looked away. He picked up a jewel-encrusted skull and held it at eye level, ostensibly pondering. "I am interested in the journey towards the Spirit," he said.

"Are you coming on to me?"

Ted smiled. He made sustained eye contact with the jewel-encrusted skull. "The case of your man, your man in the case. Does he pray or does he meditate? Does he lose the element of his corporeal form, or does his body follow him into the darkness?"

"He does just fine," Claire said. "He is a fully realized man."

"I am interested in this man Alex and his journey towards the Spirit."

"Listen, Ted. Alex lives in a suitcase. Sometimes he sticks his legs out to stretch them. Inside the suitcase, he is nude. He has a fear of commitment." She tipped back the glass of whiskey. "Honestly, I thought this meeting was going to have a different tone."

Ted turned to look at her again. "Did you think I was going to make love to you?" he asked. "You have in your possession a fully realized man."

Claire held her hand over her eyes. "No," she said. "Jesus. I have to leave, actually. I did not think you were going to do anything like that. Thank you for your time." She put down her glass and stood to leave.

Ted slipped one coaster under her glass and another under the jewel-encrusted skull. "Heaven with you," he said.

"Jesus Christ," she said. "That skull is what's strange, if you were curious."

She stopped at the hardware store on the way home. She had forgotten which light bulbs to buy and bought one of everything, and fixtures to match. She bought electric candelabras and heat lamps and mounted sconces and stand-up fixtures. She bought nightlights and Christmas lights and lamps in the Tiffany style.

At home, the suitcase snored. Claire slipped a lock on the zipper and clicked it closed. She surrounded the suitcase with lights, plugged them all into three power strips, and switched them all on at once. The suitcase made a sweet little seed pod under all that hot light. Claire wondered how it felt.

THE MOVEMENT

The end of an

As they played, the quartet at Joseph Stalin's funeral wept for another man. The tyrant lay in state, surrounded by thousands of his closest oppressed, and the greatest string quartet in Russia sat beside his casket and played beautiful music, crying for a dear friend who had died within an hour of Stalin.

The quartet, overbooked, couldn't make it to Prokofiev's funeral. Not many could, as it happened at the same time as The Great State Funeral of Joseph Stalin. It must have been harder to believe that Stalin was actually dead. This is a sign of a great man.

There were few flowers for Prokofiev's funeral, because the flower shops catered to Stalin. All Prokofiev had left in the world was thirty friends and a solo violin. Some of his friends brought flowers from home.

What they provide and how they function (present day)

The university's hall is packed, fifty more people than were at the man's own funeral. They are required to be there for credit as music majors. They try to leave at intermission but the ushers won't give them the programs they'll need as proof. They put their programs over their faces and sleep. Madeline takes her place on stage.

One little life

Madeline lives her life with the violin. She has been the concertmaster of small orchestras around the world. With her quartet, she once toured China playing Mozart, Bach, and Rolla.

Biographical note

Alessandro Rolla, teacher of Niccolò Paganini; the latter eventually would be known as one of the greatest violin players ever to have lived; cancer of the larynx would take Paganini's ability to speak, but he was heard improvising frantically on the violin on the last night of his life.

The strings no longer gut

On stage, she arranges her cropped hair, touching the frame of her glasses with a practiced hand, and raises the instrument to her neck. The strings resonate like animal gut, in a round, mellow way that any strings will sound when a master draws the bow. Her hair falls over her face as she plays the opening memorized notes of Prokofiev's last masterpiece.

Connections

1. artistic difficulty
2. distracted audience

Music theory

Playing the violin is reading and writing at once. You're given a piece in all its brilliance and insanity, ink from the same press that printed *Lolita*. The task is interpretation; it comes from the mind as easily as words.

The story is forced

Madeline left the quartet the previous summer. These days, she keeps busy by traveling too much and eating dinner at other people's houses. During private lessons, she asks her students to make up a story about the music they play. They look at the page and see the rise and fall of dynamics, the difficult fingerings and bowings, *marcato, pizzicato*. They say it's about clouds changing into different clouds, or quiet water in a well, or a boy clutching the back of a trolley car as it rumbles over the hill and off its track and plunges, out of control, into a valley. She nods, bored.

Connections (cont.)

3. representing specific emotion doesn't work in English
4. representing any emotion doesn't work in any language

General disgust

Composers show their distaste for the oppressive regime by bitching through art. In Prokofiev's case, it was twisted march songs and dissonant chords. He wrote at the physical limit of the instrument, to the upper end of the fingerboard, double trills, *sul ponticello*, muted to suffocate the solo, an accompanist jerking his head to keep time, a repeating three-bar time signature that cannot be counted and must be felt. Because of the high difficulty and low payoff, few bother to learn all four movements of his first sonata for violin.

Particular truth regarding music, life

It's an ugly, ugly piece

Little life (organization)

First movement: faux triumph
Second movement: thinly veiled mockery of Joseph Stalin
Third movement: dissonance (intentional)
Fourth movement: well,

Focused disgust

The kids in the audience don't like it. You can't blame them, really; they've been raised on the Romantics, the Baroque, the Bachs and Beethovens. Sousa never wrote an ironic note in his life. They don't understand it. They're not old enough to know the first instinct of irritation should be avoided in order to keep an open mind. The

AMELIA GRAY

violin strikes warring chords against the piano. The close listener spends most of the second movement trying to contextualize.

How to play an ugly piece

1. Change rhythms
2. Work backwards
3. Leave offerings

Context

forced marches bread lines hard winters panicked emigration mistrust genocide finger-pointing corruption occasional springtimes fire unspeakable cruelties historical insignificance wood floors broken bones icepicks dirty snow laughing women serbia the soul arthritis one tiny cold little life

How selfish of us (funerals)

The body (seen) and the person (imagined), the two reconciled into something we call an angel, a glowing light, a cool or warm breeze (depending on climate). The soul, for some reason still concerned with us, happy or appreciative at the attendance, the proper amount of tears and flowers, the quality of the entertainment and food afterwards.

Words rarely used in conversation by nineteen-year-olds

contextualize, tyrant, shudder, motif, wastrel, guttural, partition, baroque, muddy, intent, octave, cruelty

Programme

1. Attempted Explanation
2. Company of Friends
3. Sonata for Violin

At one time, Prokofiev had to have been alive

He walked through a public park. He felt snow and saw the three shades of the color grey. He took his glove off and looped his fingers around the links of a chain link fence. His hand warmed the metal and the metal chilled his hand and he thought, if the metal could feel, it would feel warm.

He thought, if the metal could feel

What if the metal could feel

It could feel warm

He thought, I wonder what Stalin is doing today. Perhaps he is having eggs, and mint tea. He thought his thoughts in Russian, which made things pleasantly guttural. He thought often of music.

Action

Madeline shudders with the final notes of the third movement. Her heavy dress is very Russian, very winter-coat. The fourth movement features runs from the opening, the theme repeated, not uncommon, but Prokofiev keeps pushing the envelope, the runs higher, confounding the lower register. The scale pattern is foreign. The upper notes approach resolution at the octave but but never arrive.

This was the piece played at Prokofiev's funeral.

AMELIA GRAY

Connections (cont)

5. no satisfying ending

The tyrant speaks

Perhaps I was having eggs, and mint tea. I tried to read the papers every morning, to be a lover of language and knowledge, but it was very tiring. I couldn't control anything outside of Russia which, if you think about it, is quite a large space outside my control. From the point of view of a man of my ambition, it is quite a large space, indeed. It is quite a large space from the point of view of any man. Anyway, I prefer coffee, and not to be recalled as a tyrant.